ANIMUS

CRIME SCENE   DO NOT ENTER

THOMAS EVANS

ANIMUS
By
Thomas Evans
Copyright © Thomas Evans 2014
Cover Illustration by C.M. Adams & Kurrie Hoyt
Published by Enigma Press
(An Imprint of Ravenswood Publishing)

GMTA Publishing Group
6296 Philippi Church Rd.
Raeford, NC 28376
http://www.gmtapublishing.com

Printed in the U.S.A.

ISBN-13: 978-0692304952
ISBN-10: 0692304959

ALSO BY THOMAS EVANS

The Hannah Books:
Hannah on the Spectrum
Hannah and Her Mommy
Hannah and Her Grandma
Hannah and Her Grandpa
Hannah and Her Best Friend
Hannah and Her One-on-One Companion

DEDICATION

This book is dedicated to my family for loving me, to my fellow writers and friends for encouraging me and to you for believing in me.
~*~

I'd like to thank all of the first responders in Cleveland County, NC for putting their lives on the line every day to protect us. Indeed a big thank you to first responders around the world for all you sacrifice and do for us.
~*~

A special thank you to the patient men and women of the Shelby and Boiling Springs, NC police departments and the Cleveland County Sherriff's department for their patience while teaching me the technical details that make this book what it is. I've always believed no mystery writer worth his or her salt may be successful without professionals they can call on for advice. I am lucky to have several entire agencies willing to walk me through the fantastic and awe-inspiring world they call 'every day.'
~*~

To C.M Adams: Sounding board, editor par excellence, cover designer, good friend and most favoritest pain in the butt. You've given me some great ideas, kept me an honest literary, and created an awesome title and a cover design that works so amazingly with your and Kurrie's art. If it hadn't been for you, this book would still be a collection of scattered thoughts rummaging around my scattered brain.

TABLE OF CONTENTS

Them that's got shall get
Them that's not shall lose
So the Bible said and it still is news
Mama may have, Papa may have
But God bless the child that's got his own
That's got his own.

-Billie Holiday

PROLOGUE

Monday, July 13, 2010 – 08:30 am:

Jason McDowell took a long drink from his beer. It was half past eight in the morning, and he was enjoying a cold one before work. "A damned shame," he said. Billy looked over to his older brother.

"A damned shame," Jason repeated, "I gotta sneak outta the house to have a beer in peace."

"Well," Billy said, finishing off his own beer. "Serves ya right for not trainin' her when ya first got her."

Jason laughed as Billy got them both fresh bottles. "Yeah," he said, twisting the top off. "But I bet ya I can teach an old dog a new trick."

"Nah," Billy said. "Gotta either beat 'em to death or get a new pup."

"Might end up doin' both," Jason said with a laugh as he finished his second beer.

"Least you can keep your bitch in the kennel," Billy said. In truth, he was glad that his wife, Joyce, was working. Not only was she doing something she loved, her income was helping them stay out of debt until he could find some work. Nevertheless, he still complained about it to his brother so Jason wouldn't think he was too weak to run his own house.

"Nah," Jason said as he stood up. "I'd rather have one earn her keep than sit around barkin' day and night."

"Yeah, well mine does earn her keep," Billy said. "Barely."

Jason looked at his brother and shook his head. "Still no luck findin' work?" he asked. Billy shook his head and opened yet another beer. "It's probably 'cause you've went through every business in town," Jason said. "Ain't nobody wants to hire you no more."

"Yeah well…" Bill didn't really have a retort, so he flipped the channel on the TV to ESPN.

"Hey," Jason said, slapping his brother's knee as he started for the door. "I'll talk to Terry when I get to work. See if he's lookin' for somebody."

"Yeah, call me and let me know," Bill said, not bothering to get his hopes up.

Jason walked out of his brother's house. His lack of attention caused him to miss the bottom step off the porch, nearly falling on his face. 'I'm not too buzzed,' he thought. 'At least I managed to stay on my feet.' He got into his pickup truck and adjusted the mirror so that he could see himself. His brown eyes were clear and not bloodshot. He was able to make out the various features of his face, a trick he learned as a teenager to judge his sobriety. He was disappointed however, to see that his two days growth of beard was showing some grey. He also saw that his once thick brown hair was starting to thin and lighten. He raked his fingers through his hair and fixed the mirror so he could see to back out. Once on the street, he put the truck in drive, spat out the window and sped down the street at twice the posted speed limit, not bothering to stop at the corner.

~*~

"Okay, girls," John Tucker said as they came back downstairs from serving his wife breakfast in bed. "Who wants to go with me to pick up Mommy's birthday cake?"

"I do, I do," Krystal squealed as she jumped up and down.

John looked at his other daughter who simply grabbed up a Dr. Seuss book and headed into the living room. Kimberly had started reading two years ago, a full year and a half before her twin sister. Since then, it became all she wanted to do. John and Janet Tucker found it an ever-increasing struggle to keep Kimberly's reading material age-appropriate. "Kimberly?" he asked.

"I'm just going to read, Daddy," the little girl said as she sat on the sofa.

"Okay," John said. "We'll be back in about twenty minutes."

"Okay," Kimberly said with a nod, only half hearing him as he and her sister walked out the door.

Five minutes later, John turned onto Second Avenue heading for the center of town. As he came to a stop at the corner, he checked the passenger-side visor mirror which he had angled to see into the back seat. Krystal was watching the scenery from her seat, barely containing her excitement. For the fourth year in a row, John and Krystal were making their annual trip to Dugan's Bakery to buy his wife, Janet, a birthday cake. For the fourth year in a row, Krystal's twin sister preferred to stay at home instead.

As he resumed his annual trek down Second Avenue, John marveled at the similarities and differences between his daughters. Identical in appearance, what with their sandy blonde hair, chocolate brown eyes and identical dimples and smiles, the two girls were as dissimilar emotionally as two people could be. For the first couple of years, John and Janet had tried buying matching clothes and dressing the girls alike, relishing the twin experience. However, for the past three years the girls began showing their independence. While Krystal liked to play and she dressed in mismatched and oddly colored clothes, Kimberly preferred to read and she normally wore one-color dresses. Janet always commented that Kimberly had an old woman's soul, while Krystal was their free spirit. Their personalities extended to their attitudes toward one another as well. The girls loved each other very much, but while Krystal always tried to engage Kimberly in her games and activities, Kimberly preferred to sit alone with her books.

This very morning in fact, when John asked his girls if they wanted to come with him to get their mother's birthday cake, he was not surprised to see Kimberly grab a book and head into the living room while her sister grabbed her shoes, one red sneaker and one black loafer.

"You know," he said as he came to another intersection, "When you start school next month, you're going to have to start wearing shoes that match."

"Why?" Krystal asked.

"Because…" he began, but couldn't finish. He didn't want to tell his little girl that the other kids might laugh at her. The last thing he wanted was to make her afraid of school. He figured Janet would find some way of tricking the girls into wearing matching outfits, at least on their first day. They continued down the street toward the bakery and John realized it would be best to let Janet figure out how to curb Krystal's unique fashion sense. As he pulled into a parking space near the entrance to the bakery, Krystal began to unbuckle her seatbelt.

"Wait until the car is off before you unbuckle," he told her for the millionth time. This was another difference in the two girls. Kimberly always waited for her parents to take the keys out of the ignition before undoing her belt.

After getting Krystal out of the car and locking the door, the two went into Dugan's Bakery hand-in-hand. Krystal inhaled deeply savoring the aroma of fresh baked pastries when they entered the bakery. She loved this smell more than she did anything else in the world. While her father went up to the register and shook hands with Mr. Dugan, Krystal made a beeline to the display case and looked in at the wonderful treats inside. "Now, if I'm not mistaken, you were just here for your birthday last week," she heard Mr. Dugan say.

"Today's Mommy's birthday," Krystal said.

"I see," Mr. Dugan said. "Well then I better get it ready." The man disappeared into the back and a few minutes later brought a box out to the front counter next to the register. "Are you ready, Kryssi?" Mr. Dugan asked her when she finally joined her dad at the register.

Krystal nodded enthusiastically. Mr. Dugan went into the back and a minute later brought out a large box and sat it on the counter. He then grabbed a stool from behind the counter and brought it out front. Once he helped the little girl onto the stool, he opened the box to show her a marvelous cake. The icing was powder blue and had a picture of her mother on the right side of it. On the left side, in gold letters were the words, "Happy Birthday, Janet." Krystal wished she knew her numbers as well as Kimberly, but with her father's help she counted the twenty-eight candles set between the lettering and her mother's picture.

"What do you think?" Mr. Dugan asked her.

"It's the best cake EVER!" the little girl squealed. Mr. Dugan laughed as he closed the box and John helped her down from the stool.

"Now," Mr. Dugan said as he tied a string around the box to keep it from opening accidentally, "Let's see what you owe me, yeah?" Krystal nodded and the man went back behind the counter to the register. "Let's see now," he said, punching some buttons. "Six hundred years of know-how, plus two weeks of really hard work, minus the pretty face I got to work with," he winked at her. "Oh! Do you have a coupon?"

"Noooo," Krystal said giggling.

"Well then," Mr. Dugan said, "We'll just have to use the

adorable-smile-discount." He cocked his eye and waited for Krystal to show him her best smile. "There we go," he said. "And your total is sixty-seven million dollars." Krystal's mouth fell open and she gawked at the baker. "But," he continued. "I will happily take sixty-seven dollars from your papa, and a million dollar hug from you.

"Deal," Krystal giggled as she reached up to give the man a hug.

When the transaction was complete, John picked up the box and turned for the door. "What do we do when Daddy's hands are full?" he asked her. When he felt the little girl grab his belt, he headed for the door. Once outside, he heard the squeal of tires and looked to the street to see a tan pickup truck swerve toward him. He dropped the cake on the sidewalk and shoved his daughter away from him.

~*~

Jason placed his elbows on the steering wheel so he could cup his hand around his cigarette and strike his lighter. Taking a deep pull from the cigarette, he tossed the lighter onto the seat beside him and turned onto Second Avenue without stopping at the sign. He took another drag before reaching back to it and trying to pull it from his lips. Unfortunately, the cigarette was stuck to his lips and he pulled his fingers down over the burning end. He jerked his hand away swearing, and let the now loose cigarette drop from his mouth. He rose up in the seat and tried feeling for it before it burned his seat and again touched the burning end.

"Dammit!" he shouted swiping at the seat and watching the cigarette fall to the floor. Bending to pick it up out of the floor, he paid no attention to his foot as it pressed down harder on the gas pedal. Once he had the cigarette back between his lips, he looked back to the road to find another car headed straight for him and pressed his foot down on the wrong pedal. Feeling his mistake, he looked down to make sure he hit the brake this time and swerved left to avoid the oncoming car.

"Fuck!" he shouted as he cut too hard and ran up onto the sidewalk. Jason McDowell did not see the man and little girl coming out of the bakery before he slammed into the wall.

Janet Tucker padded into the kitchen in her bathrobe. She sighed when she saw the remnants of the breakfast John and the girls had made her. "He could have cleaned up before they left," she mumbled. It was the same thing every year since they married. John would fix her breakfast in bed then go out for her cake and pick up some flowers. Every year, she would come downstairs to find a mess in the kitchen and would have to clean it herself. With a slight growl of frustration, she began tossing the broken eggshells into the trash and setting the dishes in the sink. She would rinse them before putting them in the washer.

"Do you want some help, Mommy?" Kimberly asked from the doorway.

"No thanks, baby," Janet, answered. "Go back to your book. This won't take long." Janet spent the next twenty minutes cleaning the kitchen and putting everything back the way she liked it. She was just about to return upstairs to change, when the doorbell rang. She checked the clock on the wall and figured it must be her mother coming over early to help set up for the party. Janet walked quickly to the door and opened it to find that it wasn't her mother, but two police officers standing on her porch.

~*~

Seven-year-old Mindy McDowell walked through the house wearing the Uncle Sam hat she got at the Fourth of July parade last week. "Mommy, can we go to the park today?" she asked as her mother sat her little brother at the table.

"Maybe after lunch," her mother answered. "We'll go for a little while, but we have to hurry home to fix supper before your daddy gets home."

"And then you have to take Auntie Joyce to work?"

"No sweetie," Angela McDowell said. "Auntie doesn't go to work until school starts back."

"How long is a little while?" Mindy asked her mother.

"About an hour or so," Angela said. She began making sandwiches for her children. While she got the bread out, she watched Mindy play with her two-year-old brother, JJ. She smiled as the little boy laughed at the girl's antics. Having two children five years apart had not exactly been her plan, but she never really planned to have any children.

Angela was once told that she would never have children. After Mindy was born, she was again told that she could not possibly conceive a second child. Five years later, Jason Junior, her second miracle-child was born. After that, Angela opted to have an operation guaranteeing no future surprises. Jason was a little put off by the decision. He loved his kids and he wouldn't mind having more, but he was mostly against having to pay the cost for the operation that would prevent them. None of it mattered now, however. The medical bills were paid off and Jason was working steadily. In a couple of years, JJ would be in school and Angela could start working again to build up a little savings. Finances may be a little tight for now, but things were looking up.

As she put the plates in front of her children, a knock came at the front door. She hated summers in Piedmont Acres. It seemed like every church in the country wanted to come around spreading the word. She really didn't have time for this today and was ready to tell them as much, when she opened the door to find two police officers waiting on the other side.

~*~

Janet jumped up from her seat as the nurse came through the door.

"How are my husband and daughter?" Janet asked.

"They're both still in surgery," the nurse said. "I just wanted to see if you needed anything while you wait."

"No, I just want to know if they'll be okay."

"Your husband took the brunt of the impact," the nurse said. "According to the witnesses, he tried to push your daughter out of the way, but she still received some substantial injuries."

"How soon will you know something?" Janet asked.

"I'll get you another update as soon as I can," the nurse said, turning to head back from where she came. Janet held her hand over her mouth to try to muffle the sobs. She held Kimberly close to her as the two waited on word.

On the same floor, but as far from Janet and Kimberly Tucker as was possible, two officers waited with Angela McDowell and her children as they, too, waited on word about their father. Angela was near panic. The officer informed her that the other two injured in the crash were a father and daughter whose conditions were grimmer than her husband's was. Angela didn't think about what she was saying when she asked if her husband had been drinking, but the officer informed her that they would be checking his blood alcohol content while he was being treated.

In the other hall, Janet and Kimberly Tucker watched as three doctors approached them. Two of them were wearing surgical scrubs. The looks on their faces caused Janet's knees to buckle and she collapsed into the chair. She didn't hear them tell her that John was dead or that her little girl was in a coma. The only thing Janet Tucker heard was her own heartbeat and even that seemed to stop for a while.

Angela McDowell heard the wail from the other side of the emergency department. No one had to tell her who it was or why. She felt her own heart wrench as the wife and mother down the hall cried out. In that moment, Angela realized her husband had destroyed two families. A doctor came over and whispered something into the officer's ear. The officer turned to Angela with a sad look on his face. "Mrs. McDowell," he said. "It looks like your husband may be charged with vehicular homicide."

Kimberly Tucker held onto her mother and buried her face in her mother's shoulder letting the woman cry, and wondering why she wasn't crying herself. Kimberly felt the fracture that the loss of her daddy and her sister caused, but still she did not cry. Kimberly sat with her mother in that hallway, comforting the adult until a doctor came back out and told them they could go to her sister.

Janet's sobs renewed when she saw her daughter lying in the hospital bed with tubes and wires going into and out of the little girl. She felt the weight of helplessness crush her as she watched her little angel being kept alive by these machines. She cried and begged Krystal to wake up and speak to her. Janet was crying still when her cellphone began ringing. The woman gave no indication she heard the phone as the ringtone continued playing from her purse. It was only from frustration that Kimberly finally dared pull the device out.

"Hello?" she said when she hit the button to answer.

"Oh hi, sweetie," the voice of her Grandma Jean, her mother's mother, came from the other end. "Now which one are you?"

"I'm Kimberly," she said quietly.

"Oh Kimmy," Grandma said. "Where's Mommy."

"We're at the hospital," Kimberly answered.

"The hospital? Why?"

"Daddy's dead."

"What?" Grandma asked. "Kimmy, are you playing? This is not a funny game."

"No," Kimberly all but whispered. "Daddy's dead and Kryssi's hurt."

"Oh my-" Grandma started. "The family is all here. Adam!" she shouted away from the receiver. "Oh God, Kimmy, Grandma's on her way."

~*~

Monday, January 11, 2011 – 06:30 am:

Janet and Kimberly left the house early that morning. This was nothing new. Since school started, Janet got Kimberly up every morning at five so they could go visit John's grave and spend an hour at the hospital visiting Krystal, before going to the school where Kimberly attended kindergarten. This morning would be different, however. When they left the hospital this morning, they would be going to the courthouse instead of school. Today was the day that Jason McDowell went on trial for killing her daddy.

Kimberly knew Jason's name and face well. He was a very important person in the Tucker household lately. Janet Tucker was obsessed with Jason McDowell. In the past six months, Janet had hired a private detective to find out as much about the man and his family as was possible. She wanted to make sure that the prosecution was armed with as much information as he could have when they started the trial.

Two months ago, the prosecutor informed Janet that he would only be able to pursue vehicular homicide charges against Jason McDowell. When she asked why he wasn't charged with drunk driving, he told her that the extent of his injuries prevented doctors from taking a BAC sample when he came into the hospital. Since he had received fresh blood during his own surgery, it was impossible to get an accurate measure of his intoxication. Any attempt to charge him with drunk driving would fall short. They had to fight the battles they could, and leave the rest to fate, he'd said.

Now, as Janet and Kimberly arrived at the courthouse, they saw that both John's parents and Janet's were already there. Janet embraced first her own mother then John's as they prepared to enter the courthouse.

"I talked to the kids last night," David Tucker, John's father, said as they stepped through the doors. "Sue and Bob will be in this afternoon. Mike will be home tomorrow."

"They all want to see this monster go to jail," John's mother, Carol, added.

"I know, Carol," Janet said as they walked through the metal detectors. "I'll just be glad when this is over and he's behind bars." The family entered the courtroom precisely at nine o'clock and waited as the lawyers entered. Soon the gallery began filling with people who had nothing better to do than to come watch the trial. None of the witnesses were allowed in the courtroom until they finished testifying, so Janet and Kimberly sat with their family and waited. At ten o'clock, with the courtroom full, the judge finally entered. After calling for order, he summoned the jury and the trial began.

The prosecutor told the jury how John Tucker was buying his wife a birthday cake the day that Jason McDowell killed him. He told them about the injuries to Krystal Tucker, John's five-year-old daughter. He explained the difficulty John's widow and other daughter were having. The prosecutor finished his speech by telling the jury that eyewitnesses smelled alcohol on Jason McDowell immediately after the accident, and he implored them to find him guilty of vehicular homicide.

The defense attorney then stood and told the jury about the faulty brake lines in the pickup truck that Jason drove that day. He told them that there was never a blood alcohol test taken on Jason so there was no proof that he drank that day. He also offered a theory that the accident was the fault of another driver who had veered into Jason's lane that day, causing him to lose control of the faulty vehicle.

For three days, Janet and her family watched as both sides argued their cases. Each day, Janet sat in the courtroom with Kimberly, her parents and John's entire family as the prosecutor presented evidence, eyewitness testimonies, character witnesses and all manner of objections and motions. She remained calm through the entire process, confident that by the end, Jason McDowell would go to jail. She sat through the defense painting McDowell as a victim himself. She listened as his brother testified that the truck he was driving needed brakes and new tires but could not afford to buy them. She sat through all of this, every day for three days, certain that she would soon see justice for her family.

The day finally arrived. On Thursday morning, both the prosecutor and defense informed the judge that they had no more to present. Judge Robert Abrams sent the jury to deliberate the case. He instructed them that they could find Jason McDowell guilty or not guilty of either vehicular homicide or the lesser charge of reckless endangerment. That statement was like a bucket of cold water thrown on Janet. No one had told her that the lesser charge was an option. She tried to get to Prosecutor O'Hare to find out what was going on, but he evaded her and left the courtroom quickly.

Janet couldn't breathe. She felt the world spinning out of control and the only thing keeping her upright was John's father holding on to her. While David led Janet out of the courthouse, he sent his son, Mike, out ahead of them. Janet was only vaguely aware of her husband's family and her own parents surrounding her in support. She only became aware of her surroundings again when Mike offered her a bottle of water.

Janet gulped the water, feeling her head clear. "What did the judge mean by 'lesser charge'?" she asked.

"He meant that even if they don't find him guilty of killing Johnny," David began, "They can still send him to jail for not being able to control his vehicle."

"I'm still confused why they didn't charge him with drunk driving," John's sister, Sue, added.

"Because when he got to the hospital," David said, "They rushed him straight into surgery. They said he'd lost so much blood, after the transfusion there wasn't enough of his own to do a proper test. He received all the clean blood in the hospital. If he had been drinking, it wouldn't have shown up, anyway."

"They couldn't test the blood on his clothes?" Sue asked.

"I guess they didn't think about it," David said.

"It's not that easy," Mike said. "It's not like on TV. Even if they had tested his clothes, there's no guarantee they would have found alcohol and if they had, there could have been any number of explanations for it showing up without him being drunk. Even a fat idiot like Winslow would have torn that evidence to shreds."

~*~

"How long do you think it's gonna take?" Jason asked his lawyer.

"Hard to tell," Martin Winslow said. "I feel like O'Hare petered out at the end there and we did offer a compelling argument."

"Is that why he agreed to reckless endangerment?" Angela asked.

"Probably," Winslow said. "I couldn't get him to give us a plea bargain. At least the reckless endangerment charge gives us some padding."

"How is another charge paddin'?" Jason asked.

"Even if the jury didn't believe you were responsible for Tucker's death," Winslow said, "They might think you were guilty of negligence or failing to control your vehicle. Therefore, instead of letting you off for homicide, they might find you guilty just so they could punish you for something. The reckless endangerment charge gives them an option to find you guilty of something smaller so they won't have to find you guilty of the greater charge."

"And what if they find me guilty of both?" Jason asked.

"I didn't say it wasn't a gamble."

"What?" Jason asked with a puzzled look.

"Look," Winslow said, "With everything they've heard, the jury could go in there more confused than when they came out. They could spend days in there sorting through the testimonies and evidence before they decided that you weren't guilty of any wrong doing, but then again, they could just get frustrated and find you guilty of one or both charges."

"How could they find him guilty of both?" Angela asked.

"Well technically they can't," Winslow said. "The judge's instructions were for them to find him guilty or not guilty of one or the other. Sometimes juries get confused and they try to find someone guilty of both charges offered. If they try that, the judge will send them back to decide of which charge they find you guilty. If they do that, they may opt for the more severe one."

"So why offer the lesser charge at all if it gets them confused?" Angela asked.

"Because it is a gamble," Winslow said. "O'Hare knows the odds are in his favor, which is why he offered it. However, sometimes the jury chooses the lesser charge."

"So it's not likely he'll get off?"

"It depends on how closely the jury paid attention. And, if they didn't pay close attention, it will depend on how thoroughly they go back through the evidence."

"So gamblin' odds..." Jason said.

"Four to one against," Winslow said.

"But wait, a minute ago you seemed pretty confident," Angela said.

"Yeah," said Jason.

"I'm paid to seem confident. I'm also obligated to be honest with you. If this jury is lazy, you could go to jail."

"Mother-"

"Jason, not here," Angela interrupted her husband.

"Let's just grab some lunch while we wait," Winslow said, as he moved to lead them from the courthouse grounds.

~*~

The Tucker family took up the two front rows behind the prosecutor's table. It was just after lunch when the bailiff informed them that the jury had reached a decision. Now, all of the Tuckers shifted their gazes from the defense table to the jury box. It seemed to take forever before the judge banged his gavel and brought the court to order.

"Has the jury reached a verdict?" the judge asked.

A woman stood up in the jury box and said, "We have, Your Honor,"

"In the case of the people versus Jason McDowell," the judge said, "How do you find on the charge of vehicular homicide?"

"Not guilty," the woman said. A gasp went through the gallery. Janet Tucker began sobbing. The judge again banged his gavel, bringing quiet back into the courtroom.

"In the above name action, how do you find the defendant on the charge of reckless endangerment?" the judge asked.

"Not guilty."

The gallery erupted with outrage. It took several moments of pounding his gavel before the judge could restore order to the courtroom. When at last the only sound in the courtroom was the quiet sobs of Janet Tucker, the judge spoke again.

"Jason McDowell," he began with a shocked expression on his face, "You have been found not guilty of the charges levied against you. While many may not agree with the decision, by law a jury of your peers has found you innocent. You are now free to go. This case is adjourned."

The banging of the gavel acted as a signal for Janet. Her sobs stopped cold and her head snapped up. She rose from her seat and looked directly at the jury. "He killed my husband!" she shouted. "He put my daughter in a coma! He was driving drunk and destroyed my family, and you're letting him get away with everything!" The judge banged his gavel repeatedly calling for order as Adam Greene tried to escort his daughter out of the courtroom. "You're all helping him get away with murder and you don't care!" Janet screamed as her father pulled her out of the courtroom. "You son of a bitch!" she screamed at Jason just before the doors closed on her.

Once in the hallway, Janet broke down into convulsing sobs, leaning on her father for support. Kimberly held her mother's hand as the woman wept. She turned to look at the courtroom door as it opened and Jason McDowell stepped out with his wife. The man spared a glance at the little girl and smiled before his lawyer ushered them down the hall. Kimberly stared after them, a look of pure hatred on her young face.

~*~

Janet's mother finally got her calmed enough to leave the courthouse. Fifteen minutes later, they pulled into the driveway on Palmetto Drive. Adam practically carried his daughter into the house as his wife and granddaughter followed. John's parents and siblings stayed with them until late in the evening, sharing their disbelief in the verdict. It wasn't until Mike pointed out that they could do no more, that reality finally sank in. Soon, one-by-one, they began to leave, giving Janet and Kimberly time alone.

"Wanna help me pick out something for school tomorrow?" Kimberly asked her mother.

Janet looked up at her and smiled. "I know you miss school, baby," she said. "But how about you and I spend one more day together? You can wait until Monday to go back, can't you?"

Kimberly nodded enthusiastically. Even though she wanted to

go back to school tomorrow, she knew her mother needed her more. Maybe she could talk her mommy into going to the park or something tomorrow. As she watched her mother go upstairs, still crying, Kimberly grabbed up a book and got ready to read it until bedtime. Walking into the kitchen, she noticed the mess from earlier and thought about reminding her mother that it needed to be cleaned. Looking to the ceiling as if she were lookin to her mother's room, she reconsidered.

Kimberly put the book on the counter and began scraping the plates into the sink before placing them into the dishwasher. Once the machine was loaded, she got one of the washer tabs from under the sink and placed it in its cup before closing and starting the wash cycle. Soon, she had rinsed the scraps down into the disposal and wiped off the counters and table. Once done, she laid the towel on the table and grabbed her book back up.

Kimberly was snuggled into her father's chair with his lamp turned on when she noticed the box in front of the fireplace. Curious, she got up and went over to examine it. Inside were the files and documents her mother had collected about Jason McDowell over the past six months. Kimberly shuffled through the papers for a while before putting them back into the box and closing the lid.

She stood thinking for a moment. Realizing that this box could upset her mother tomorrow, Kimberly decided to put it away. She lugged the heavy box over to the basement door, and one-step at a time dragged it downstairs. Once in the basement, she dragged the box to her father's workbench and slid it underneath. That final job complete, she rushed back upstairs and snuggled once again into her daddy's chair to read her book until bedtime. It was in her father's chair that Janet found her the next morning.

~*~

Jason McDowell spent his night celebrating. He and Billy managed to drink a case of Ice House before Angela and Billy's wife, Joyce, put an end to the festivities. The women had to be at work the next morning, Joyce at the school, and Angela at the supermarket, so they made the guys cut out the frivolity so they could get some sleep.

"Now that I got out from under this shit," Jason said as Billy slipped him a beer, "She is gonna get outta that damned store. And then she's gonna get her ass back home."

"I thought you said you'd rather have her workin' than layin' around the house all day," Billy said with a laugh.

"That was before I got fired and she started lordin' it over me that she was earnin' and I ain't." Jason said, taking a drink from his beer.

"You know what I think?" Billy asked.

"What?"

"I think you should make her keep the job."

Jason looked at his brother. "What?"

"Just listen," Billy said. "Joyce is still teachin' school, even though I'm workin' steady at the mill right?"

"Yeah."

"Well, between the two of us we're almost out of debt," he said. "We only got three more payments on the house, the car's paid off and the truck almost is, too. Hell, she's even talkin' 'bout goin' to the beach or somethin' next summer."

"That's fine for you," Jason said. "Joyce ain't got two kids to watch. She can lay out all day."

"Dude," Billy said, "Mindy is in school all day, and Angie puts JJ in that daycare."

"Yeah," Jason scoffed, "But, she should be the one watchin' him."

"Man, let him stay in the daycare 'til y'all get above-ground. Then after you're out of debt, you can put her ass home if you want."

"I don't know, man," Jason said, taking a long drink.

"Trust me, man," Billy said. "They said you could have the house back if you got the back rent paid up didn't they?"

"I guess," Jason said. "If I get back to work quick enough, we can get it back before they put somebody else in it."

"Then this is the quickest way to do it."

The two of them continued lounging on the sofa, Jason drinking and Billy pretending to. By morning, Billy had his brother convinced that keeping Angela working was a good idea. Billy figured with both of them working, they could soon get back into their own place and he and Joyce would have their house to themselves again.

~*~

ONE

Monday, August 26, 2013 – 04:30 am:

Kimberly Tucker checked herself in the mirror before grabbing her backpack and heading downstairs. As she descended the stairs, she heard her mother in the kitchen preparing breakfast. Walking in, she saw that her mother was still in her bathrobe.

"Mom," she said, concerned by her mother's appearance. "We're going to be late."

"Honey, it's four-thirty in the morning," Janet said. "You'll be at school in plenty of time."

"Not if we stop by the cemetery and the hospital."

"I thought we'd skip the cemetery today," Janet said, sitting down across from her daughter.

"What?"

"Honey," she began, taking hold of her eight-year-old daughter's hand. "For three years, we have spent an hour every morning at the cemetery doing nothing more than just looking at a headstone and wishing it weren't there." She held up her hand when she saw Kimberly start to protest. "I know that you don't mind going. You are such a sweet child to put up with me through all of this, but it's time I let you be just that, a child.

"We're still going to visit your sister every morning," she continued, "But at least we get to sleep in an extra hour, yeah?"

"Yeah," Kimberly agreed and hugged her mother.

"Now," Janet said going over to the coffee maker. "You are

starting fifth grade. Nervous?"

"Nope," Kimberly said. "I met Mrs. Estep last year. She seems nice."

"Planning on skipping another grade this year?"

"Maybe," Kimberly said. "It depends on how hard the work is."

"I have faith in you, baby," Janet said as the two of them dug into their breakfasts.

Across town on Willowood Lane, Mindy McDowell was just waking up. Like Kimberly, Mindy would be starting fifth grade today. Unlike Kimberly, Mindy had not skipped any grades to get there. The ten-year-old took a quick shower and dressed before going into her little brother's room. JJ would be starting his first day of kindergarten today and Mindy wanted to go with him when their mother introduced him to his teacher.

Mindy quietly made her way to JJ's bed and sat down on the edge before gently shaking his shoulder. "Wake up, sleepy head," she whispered with a quick shake. The little boy's eyes sprang open and he sat up quickly.

"Min?" he asked rubbing his eyes. "Is it time for school?"

"Just about," Mindy said. "Come on, get ready and I'll get us some breakfast."

She made sure her brother got out of bed before making her way downstairs. She barely noticed the unconscious forms of her father and uncle on the sofa as she entered the kitchen. She had cereal poured for herself and JJ when her aunt and mother arrived downstairs. Mindy heard her mother's grunt of disgust before they came into the kitchen, but ignored it in hopes that the targets of her scorn would remain asleep until they left.

"Good morning, Min," her Aunt Joyce said as she turned on the coffee maker.

"Good morning, Miss McDowell," Mindy chanted just as she had to do every morning last year when her aunt was her teacher.

"Very funny," her aunt said with a smile.

"What's funny?" JJ asked as he came into the kitchen.

"Your sister with a Fruit Loop in her nose," Joyce said, eliciting a giggle from her nephew.

"Shh," Angela admonished them.

"JJ," Mindy said before taking another bite of cereal. "Remember you can't call Auntie Joyce 'Auntie' at school."

"I know," he said. "But everyone knows she's my aunt."

"Doesn't matter," Mindy said. "You still have to call her Miss McDowell."

"Fine," JJ said.

"What time do you get off work?" Joyce asked Angela.

"Three if everyone shows up on time," her sister-in-law answered.

The four of them finished breakfast and then filed out to the Buick, which Angela had previously owned. She sold it to Joyce when Jason lost his job three years earlier. Being out of work and the expense of the trial had caused them to lose the Buick, their home, and just about everything else but their clothes and Jason's truck. Billy and Joyce allowed them to move in with them, but

Angela knew that this arrangement couldn't last much longer.

Jason had a job now and between the two of them, they were working hard to pay off their debts and get their own place again. Her plan was for her and Jason to have their own house sometime before Christmas. Of course, that depended on Jason actually keeping this job. He had been unable to keep a job for longer than a month or two, since the trial a couple of years ago. With his constant drinking and belligerent attitude, few employers were willing to put up with him.

The pretty, little Latina continued to soap the window of his pickup making sure to lean close enough to it that she wet her shirt. Jason had had more than enough and lowered the window. "Why don't you go ahead and climb in here," he said. "We can get something else good and clean." She opened the door and climbed in, straddling him as she moved over to the passenger seat. Once she was on the passenger side, she sat up on her knees and began unbuttoning his shirt while he reached over to caress her.

"What's yer name, baby?" he asked.

"Jase," she said.

"What?"

"Jase, wake up!" she said again shaking his shoulder. Jason's eyes opened to see his brother nudging him awake.

"What?" he snapped.

"Here," Billy said, handing him the phone. "And get yer hand off my titty."

Jason jerked his hand from his brother's chest and grabbed the phone. "What?" he snapped to the caller.

"McDowell," the voice of Jim Cremeans, his supervisor, came over the line. "You were supposed to be here two hours ago."

"Shit," Jason said, rubbing his eyes. "I slept through the alarm. Let me get a shower and I'll be there in a half hour."

"Don't even bother with it," Jim said. "But Mr. Ramey said you'd better have a good excuse when you come to work tomorrow."

"Fuck him," Jason said.

"Jase," Jim said.

"Tell him I'll be there in half an hour." Jason said and pushed the disconnect button.

"You sure you want to piss him off like that?" Billy asked.

"He ain't nothin'," Jason said staggering to his feet. As Jason made his way upstairs to the shower, Billy got up and headed for the kitchen. Today was his day off, so he would just have a cup of coffee and then go back to sleep.

Billy had barely finished half a cup of coffee when he heard Jason trample down the stairs and head out the door. 'Bastard's gonna get fired again,' he thought. 'They ain't never gettin' the hell outta here.' Finishing his coffee, he checked the refrigerator and saw he was out of beer.

"She better grab some on her way home," he said to himself. "Or he'll be showin' his ass and I might just put all of them out."

Billy made his way back through the living room to the front hall and climbed up the stairs. He made it to the top landing and noticed Jason's towel and dirty clothes lying in the bathroom and hallway floor. He grumbled as he picked up after his brother. After throwing the clothes into the hamper, he went to his bedroom and fell onto the bed. He was asleep less than a minute later.

Mindy and Angela watched as Mrs. Black, the kindergarten teacher, led JJ into the classroom. The boy had barely gotten inside when two other boys came up to him and led him over to the play area. Mindy smiled at them before turning with her mother and heading down the hall to her own class. She kissed her mother goodbye outside the classroom and headed in to talk to her friend Lesley, who was already inside.

"Hey," Lesley said as Mindy entered the classroom. "You're here early."

"Yeah, we brought JJ in to meet his teacher," Mindy said.

"You will not believe what happened to Kelly this summer," Lesley said.

The two girls were still sharing gossip from their classmates when Kimberly walked in and handed Mrs. Estep her paperwork.

"Min," Lesley whispered. "That's her."

"Who?" Mindy asked looking at the new arrival.

"That's the girl who skipped two grades," Lesley said. She was in Robbie's class last year because she skipped second grade, now she's in our class because she skipped fourth."

"She looks scared," Mindy said.

Kimberly was scared. When she walked in, she saw the girls sitting together and immediately recognized the taller brunette from the files her mother collected. She should have realized that she would be sharing a classroom with Jason McDowell's daughter this year, but for some reason it never occurred to her.

Mrs. Estep looked over the paperwork and tucked it into her drawer. "It looks like you're determined to skip every other grade, Miss Tucker," the teacher said. "Do you plan to test out of sixth grade at the end of the year?"

"Yes, ma'am," Kimberly said.

"Well, I hope we can keep up with you," Mrs. Estep said. "Go over there and get one of each book and put your name in the front. We still have a half an hour before class starts, so if you want, you can introduce yourself to the students who are already here."

"Yes, ma'am," Kimberly said again, heading over to the stacks of textbooks.

Kimberly had barely gotten her third book before the McDowell girl and her friend came over and started getting her own books.

"Hi," the shorter girl said, holding out her hand. ."I'm Lesley Bennett, and this is Mindy McDowell."

"Kimberly Tucker," Kimberly said shaking each girl's hand in turn. She was surprised and annoyed that the name didn't seem to mean anything to Mindy.

"So, you're the one who skipped two grades right?" Lesley asked.

"Yeah," Kimberly said as she got the last of her books.

"Wanna sit with us?" Mindy asked. Kimberly shrugged and the two girls, having gotten their own books led her over to their desks.

"So Kim," Lesley said. "Are your mom and dad like super smart too?

"It's Kimberly, and not really," Kimberly answered. "I mean my mom's smart, but she never skipped any grades. Neither did my dad, but he was pretty smart too."

"So is it like you automatically know everything?" Mindy asked.

"No," Kimberly said. "I still have to learn everything, but I usually learn it all from reading."

"You must love to read," Lesley said as she started writing her name in her books.

"Yeah," Kimberly said. "And I read a lot faster than most people.

"Like how fast?" Mindy asked.

Kimberly thought for a minute as she looked over her textbooks. "I'll probably have all of these read by Friday," she told them. "And by the time I read through them again, I'll have everything memorized."

"Seriously?" Mindy and Lesley said together. Kimberly nodded and the two girls looked at one another and mouthed the word, 'wow'.

"So do you want to be my new best friend?" Lesley asked.

"Forget that," Mindy said. "We'll throw Lesley out the window and you can be my new best friend." In spite of herself, Kimberly found herself laughing with the two girls, an event that did not go unnoticed by Mrs. Estep. The three girls continued laughing and talking until they heard the first bell ring. Kimberly was surprised to find the class suddenly full of students. She hadn't noticed them coming in.

~*~

Janet sat in the chair next to Krystal's bed. As was her routine, she returned to the hospital after dropping Kimberly off at school. They had already visited this morning before school and would return later, after Janet picked the girl up. For now, Janet sat beside her daughter's bed and watched, hoping for some indication that her little girl was coming back to her. She began talking to her, telling her again about the plans she had for when Krystal came out of her coma. She planned a vacation that would last all summer, and would cook all of the little girl's favorite foods. Just as she was telling Krystal about the party she planned to throw for her, Krystal's doctor and the hospital administrator came in.

"Mrs. Tucker," Dr. Adams, the administrator, said as he and Dr. Satish took the other two seats in the room. "I just received a fax from EquiSure. It seems they are no longer willing to pay all of Krystal's care expenses."

"I don't understand," Janet said. "The policy is still good, isn't it?"

"Yes," Dr. Adams said. "You, Krystal and Kimberly are still fully insured, but EquiSure believes that it is no longer viable to cover Krystal's continued care."

"So they're just not going to pay any more?"

"No," Dr. Satish said. "She will still receive coverage for her stay and treatments."

"Provided she remains a patient," Dr. Adams added.

"What do you mean?" Janet asked.

"EquiSure is discontinuing their coverage of Krystal's stay," Dr. Adams said. "They believe that after three years, she would be better served in a dedicated care facility or at home…"

"Or she's in a condition where it won't matter," Dr. Satish finished with disdain.

"Doctor Satish, please," Dr. Adams said. Turning back to Janet, he continued, "Mrs. Tucker, we believe that Krystal is getting the best care here, and we have assured EquiSure that she is in the best possible environment."

"So what is the problem?"

"I'm afraid that that EquiSure disagrees," Dr. Adams said. "Without some positive indicators, we need to look at alternative care."

"What do you mean 'positive indicators'?" Janet asked, her disgust starting to show.

"I mean unless Krystal starts showing some signs of coming out of the coma, we would not be able to keep her at the hospital. We'll have to send her to another facility."

"What kind of facility?"

"A long-term care facility," Dr. Adams said quickly, "Most

likely a nursing home."

"No," Janet said, shaking her head. "My daughter is not going into a nursing home."

"There is also the alternative to care for her at home," Dr. Satish supplied. "I'm not sure how your insurance company would feel about that, but it is the least expensive, safe alternative."

"Safe alternative?" Janet asked.

"I think that EquiSure would be happy to have you throw her in a ditch. That way she wouldn't incur any expenses and they wouldn't have to pay anything. Companies like that don't care for the patients, just the bottom line."

"That is enough, doctor!" Adams snapped.

"Enough what?" Janet asked. "Enough of him being honest? Of telling me the truth about how my insurance company feels about the life of my daughter?"

"Mrs. Tucker," Dr. Adams said. "Although we may not agree with EquiSure, by law our hands are tied. Unless you are able to take over the cost of her care out of pocket, we are required to seek other arrangements by the end of the week."

"We'll see about that," Janet said, standing up and grabbing her purse.

"Mrs. Tucker," Dr. Adams called after her. When she disappeared around the corner, he rounded on Dr. Satish. "If she tries to sue the hospital because of you-"

"What would you do if it were your daughter?" Satish asked him and left Dr. Adams in the room with the little girl he planned to send to a nursing home. Doctor Adams looked at the girl, sighed and shook his head before leaving as well.

~*~

Joyce McDowell looked out over the playground making sure all of her students were in sight. Doing a quick head count, she was satisfied that they were all there and safe, so she turned again to the three girls sitting on the bench beside the playground. Her niece, Mindy, was easy to spot, and Lesley Bennett was never far from Mindy at school. The girl that caught her attention was the small blonde that sat with them.

For the first time in their lives, Joyce noted, Mindy and Lesley had their textbooks out and were reading them during recess. 'It must be the new girl's influence,' she mused. "Heather," she called aloud to Mrs. Estep, Mindy's teacher. Mrs. Estep came closer and Joyce asked, "Is that who I think it is with Mindy and Lesley?"

"That's Kimberly Tucker," Mrs. Estep said.

"Oh my God," Joyce said.

"Don't worry," Mrs. Estep said, holding up a hand. "They don't seem to know."

"They'll eventually find out," Joyce said.

"Maybe," Mrs. Estep replied. "But I don't think they really paid much attention to the details of the trial. Plus it's been three years."

"Still…"

"Don't worry, Joyce," Mrs. Estep said. "They were fast friends. I'll keep an eye out if anything develops. Besides, if Miss Tucker has her way, this will be the only year they will share classes."

"Sometimes I feel like she studied so hard just to skip my class personally."

"Don't be silly," Mrs. Estep said with a laugh. "Let them be, it'll be okay."

"I hope you're right."

While Joyce divided her attention between the trio of girls and her own class, she began feeling quite sleepy. After her second yawn, it occurred to her that she should check her blood sugar. Bringing out her meter, she pierced her finger and allowed a drop of blood to fall onto the strip. After about a minute, the machine beeped and she noted her blood glucose level was 175 mg/dL. 'Crap,' she thought.

"Heather," she called again, walking over to the woman. "I hate to do this, but can you herd my class for me while I go take a shot?"

"Are you okay?" Mrs. Estep asked.

"Yeah," Joyce said. "It just snuck up on me."

"Go on," Mrs. Estep said. "I got 'em."

As Joyce headed back into the building, Mrs. Estep scanned the playground making sure she knew where every one of her own and Joyce's students were.

~*~

"Mike, please! There has to be something you can do," Janet spoke through her tears.

"I'll try," Mike Tucker said as he picked up his phone. "I may not be able to get EquiSure to change their minds, but maybe I can get the hospital to hold off while I try."

"Please, Mike," Janet sobbed. "I can't bear the thought of sending her to a nursing home."

Mike spoke into the phone for a few moments, then dialed another number. After about half an hour's worth of phone calls, he hung up and looked at Janet with a smile. "Okay, sis," he said as he stood up. "I have good news and bad news. Judge Hartnett is giving us an injunction preventing the hospital from sending Krystal to another facility until we can get a hearing with EquiSure."

"What's the bad news?" Janet asked.

"EquiSure wants to see us today."

"What?"

"I need to serve the hospital with the injunction, and then we can head over there."

"But isn't this a little quick?"

"I hope not," Mike said as they left his office.

An hour later, after serving the injunction papers to the hospital administrator, Mike Tucker walked into the offices of Jerry Hastings, the Piedmont Acres agent for EquiSure Insurance Company.

"Mike, Janet," Jerry said as they entered his office. "They're set to call in the next few minutes."

"You know what this is all about, right?" Mike asked.

"Yeah," Jerry said. "It's a damned shame, Mike. Janet, I'm so sorry."

"Don't be sorry, Jerry," Janet said. "Just try to fix it."

"We're gonna try," Jerry said as his phone rang. "That's them."

After a cursory greeting between Jerry and the main office for EquiSure, the negotiations began in earnest.

"You must understand, Mr. and Mrs. Tucker, that the costs of a continued hospital stay are outstanding. The nutrition supplements alone have cost us nearly two-hundred thousand dollars."

"What about less expensive alternatives?" Jerry asked.

"If the patient can be placed in a long term facility-"

"You mean a nursing home." Janet interrupted.

"Yes, ma'am," the representative said. "EquiSure can continue to pay half of the costs of her treatments. The balance of which would need to be paid by you."

"Why only half?" Janet asked.

"The patient's condition does not have a positive prognosis," the representative said. "Statistically, coma patients very rarely awaken to lead normal, healthy lives, especially after such a long time. According to the patient's medical records, there is no indication that she will emerge from the coma in the foreseeable future. And if she does, there is still no indication of how much damage has been done to the brain."

"What about in-home care?" Jerry asked.

"In-home care is of course the least expensive alternative," the representative answered. "The patient will receive a monthly allotment for physical therapy and medications. However, nutrition and any additional therapy and medications will have to come out of pocket. Additionally, the patient-"

"Can you stop calling her that?" Janet interrupted.

"Excuse me?"

"Her name is Krystal," Janet said. "Not 'the patient'."

"I'm very sorry, ma'am," the representative said. "I meant no disrespect."

"Fine," Janet said. "What is the bottom line?"

It took nearly half an hour of arguing from Mike, and pleas from Janet, but ultimately EquiSure remained firm on their position and urged Janet to consider all of her options and prepare to move her daughter by the end of the week.

"Mrs. Tucker," the representative said before Jerry could end the call. "I'm aware that the expenses involved will be heavy, and I apologize for that. You might want to look into getting government assistance to help offset these costs."

"Thank you," Janet said. "But I would rather let the government give assistance to those who truly need it. I will cover my daughter's expenses myself."

~*~

Angela walked into the house frustrated that her boss had sent her home early. She really didn't like the little snot, especially since he became her assistant manager. It seemed that he kept giving the better schedules to the employees he socialized with outside of work. This left the older employees who had been there a few years to pick up the few remaining hours. If he gave her another short day like this, she would have to pawn her wedding ring again to make sure she had enough gas to get her and Joyce to work the next week.

"You're home early," Jason said as she walked into the living room. "Just as good. Grab me another beer and fix me a sandwich."

"What are you doing home?" she asked.

"Huh?" he grunted paying more attention to the fishing show on TV than to her.

"I said 'what are you doing home,'" she repeated.

"Oh," he said. "That peckerwood, Bert Ramey got his panties in a bind."

"Why?" Angela asked.

"I slept through the alarm this mornin' and Jim called me, chewin' me out," Jason said, turning to give her a puzzled look. "Where the hell's my beer?"

"So Bert sent you home early?"

"Get me my damned beer!" he snapped.

"How late were you?" she asked.

"A couple of hours, shit!" he said. "Now will you get me the damned beer?"

"No!"

"What?" He asked turning around.

"I said 'no,'" she replied. "You were up drinking all night and slept in this morning. You're not going to sleep in and be late tomorrow, too."

"I'm not goin' in tomorrow," he said. "Now get me the damned beer."

Angela gave him a disgusted look and asked, "Did you get suspended?"

"No the asshole fired me!"

"What?"

"Jim called and chewed me out and told me that I had to have an excuse for Bert tomorrow and I said 'fuck Bert,'" Jason told her. "The asshole had me on speaker and Bert waited till I drove all the way over there, and fired me."

"God dammit, Jason!" she shouted as she stomped into the kitchen. "We're barely able to pay the bills we have now! How in the hell are we going to get our own place with you getting fired every other month?"

She came back into the living room with his beer to find him rolling his eyes and flapping his hand, mimicking her. Anger overtook her and she flung the can at him, hitting him in the back of the head. As soon as the can left her hand, she realized her mistake and turned to run, but not quickly enough. Jason jumped from the sofa and lunged for her.

"Throw a fuckin' beer can at me?" he yelled as the first punch landed on the back of her head and sent her sprawling. "Who the fuck do you think you are?" he yelled as he kicked her in the side. Her whimpering stopped short as the air left her and she felt him grab her hair, lifting her off of the floor. "You think because I let you keep that job you can start actin' any way you want? Here's what you get for thinkin' like that!" The tears running down her cheeks blurred her vision so Angela did not see the punch as it landed on her cheek. Her head snapped so quickly that she was unconscious before the second or third punches caught her jaw and nose.

~*~

Joyce McDowell was starting to worry. She, her niece, and her nephew waited on the steps of the school for her sister-in-law to come pick them up. Since Joyce taught at the school, neither child rode the bus. They always came to school with her. Unfortunately, she now shared a car with Angela, who took it to work today. Normally, if she expected to work late, Angela would come to school on her break and Joyce would take her back to work before taking the kids home, but approaching three-thirty there was still no sighting of the car or Angela.

At a quarter till four, Principal Lloyd Moore left the building and stopped to ask her if he could take them home. She knew Billy wasn't the jealous type, but she still avoided any situation where she would be alone with another man, even one she worked with. She thanked Lloyd and turned him down, opting to wait for Angela. Forty-five minutes later, she was starting to panic. She took the kids back inside and went to the custodian's office where Sue Middleton, the head custodian sat working on a supply order.

"Sue," Joyce said as she knocked on the door.

"Oh, Mrs. McDowell," Sue said as she looked up. "I thought you had left."

"Not yet," Joyce said. "It looks like my sister-in-law is running late. Can I use your phone to call a taxi?"

"Don't be silly. I'll run you home," Sue told her.

"I can't ask you to do that."

"Please," Sue said. "It's almost time for my break anyway, and this order can wait."

"Thank you," Joyce said with a sigh of relief.

Ten minutes later, they pulled to the curb in front of the McDowell house on Willowood Lane. Joyce was annoyed to see her car parked beside Jason's pickup. After thanking Sue and offering her a couple of dollars for driving them home, Joyce ushered the children up the sidewalk to the house. When she opened the door she saw Angela lying on the floor, and closed the door again quickly. Turning to the children, she told them to go around to the back door and she would let them in there.

Mindy grabbed her brother's hand and led him around back as Joyce opened the door again and ran to her sister-in-law who was lying on the floor crying. She could see blood caked on Angela's face and her eye was starting to swell. She looked and saw Jason sitting on the sofa in the living room, watching TV.

"Hold on," Joyce whispered to Angela before running into the kitchen to open the back door for the kids. "Okay, you two," she said. "I want you to both stay in here until I tell you otherwise. Mindy, make a sandwich for both of you. I'll be right back."

As she made her way back into the hall, she cast a malevolent glance at Jason while he continued drinking a beer and watching the TV. "What did you do to her?" she asked him as she leaned down to check on Angela.

"You might want to be careful," he said. "I'd hate to have to tell Billy why yer layin' there with her."

"Son of a bitch," she whispered. "Angie, honey, can you get up?" she asked, trying to turn the other woman over.

"JJ and Mindy," Angela moaned.

"They're in the kitchen," Joyce whispered. We need to get you to the hospital." To Jason she said, "Can you at least call an ambulance?"

"I'm fine," he said. "My head's quit hurtin' now."

"Angie," she whispered again. "Can you get up? I'm going to take you to the hospital, okay?"

"Don't leave the kids here alone," Angela moaned.

"Okay," Joyce said. "I'll be right back." Joyce left Angela lying in the floor while she ran back into the kitchen.

"What's wrong, Auntie?" Mindy asked her. Joyce pulled the girl to the corner of the kitchen and started whispering.

"Your mom's been hurt. I need you to take JJ out to the car and get him buckled into his seat while I get your mama out there. Keep him distracted so he doesn't see her. We have to take her to the hospital."

Mindy nodded and grabbed her jacket from the counter. "JJ, come on, we're going for a ride," she said.

"Is Auntie coming?" he asked.

"Yeah," Mindy said as she helped him into his own jacket and grabbed the car keys from the counter.

Once the kids were out the back door, Joyce returned to Angela's side. "Billy!" she called looking up the stairs.

"He ain't here," Jason said as he got up to go into the kitchen.

"Where is he?" Joyce asked.

"Mill called him in to work the late shift," Jason answered. "He'll be home by nine though. You gonna start supper?" Joyce gave her brother-in-law a look of disgust as she struggled to help Angela to her feet.

~*~

Janet and Kimberly walked into Krystal's room to find Dr. Satish standing over the comatose child. When he saw them enter, he smiled and nodded. After a few minutes, he finished checking Krystal's monitors and walked over to them.

"Mrs. Tucker," he said. "I am terribly sorry about this morning."

"It wasn't your fault, doctor," Janet said. "You were honest with me, and I believe you really care about Krystal. I'm just worried about what happens next."

"Well, we've run some tests," Dr. Satish said. "I can't make any promises, but I think everything will be fine."

"I'm going to get together with both of her grandfathers and her uncle. We're going to go over the finances to see if it would be feasible to bring her home," Janet said. "If that is possible, could we make an arrangement for you to come by and check on her periodically?"

"Mrs. Tucker, there is no need to make an arrangement," Dr.

Satish said. "I would be happy to stop by on my way home from work to check on her if you are able to bring her home."

"Thank you, doctor," Janet said.

"I can also get you the number to a good medical supply company."

"Thank you," Janet said. "I think I should wait to make sure first."

"Of course," Dr. Satish said. "I have some other patients to check in on, but if you have any more questions just have me paged."

Janet thanked him again as he left. Kimberly, meanwhile, had walked over to her sister's bed. "It's going to be okay," she whispered. "You're not going to have to be in here much longer."

Janet and Kimberly spent nearly an hour talking to Krystal, reassuring her and themselves that everything was going to be okay. Mother and daughter both knew the reassurances were more for each other than for Krystal. As they were leaving, Dr. Satish caught up to them and gave Janet several pamphlets and documents.

"These will explain almost everything you're facing," the doctor told her. "It gives you details on some of the care facilities in the area and lets you know what to expect if you decide on in-home care. And I went ahead and made a list of some of the stuff you will need with a list of places you can get them inexpensively."

Janet thanked him one final time and handed the information

packets to Kimberly while she fished the car keys out of her purse. Once outside, Kimberly started looking the pamphlets over until she heard a familiar voice from the other end of the sidewalk.

"JJ, get out of the way," Mindy said as a woman brought a wheelchair to the car they were standing by. Kimberly recognized the woman as Mrs. McDowell, the fourth grade teacher at her school. She knew the teacher wasn't Mindy's mother since she knew Angela McDowell's face from the hearing three years earlier. Kimberly watched as Mrs. McDowell helped someone climb from the car and into the waiting wheelchair. She started walking over to the group when her mother called her name.

"Hold on, Mommy," Kimberly said. "I know them."

Janet followed Kimberly to the group and waited while her daughter spoke to the dark haired girl and little boy.

"Mindy," Kimberly said startling the girl. "Is everything okay?"

Mindy looked at her new friend and the tears she was holding back began falling. "My mommy's been hurt," the older girl said.

"I hope she'll be okay," Kimberly said. "I wish I could stay with you, but we have to go."

"It's okay," Mindy said. "I'll tell you everything at school tomorrow."

"Okay," Kimberly said. "I hope your mom feels better."

"Thanks," Mindy answered as she and her brother followed her mother and aunt into the hospital.

"Who was that?" Janet asked as Kimberly rejoined her.

"A friend from school," Kimberly answered. She didn't want to upset her mother by letting her find out that her new friend was the daughter of the man who had killed her father.

"Oh," Janet said. "I hope everything's alright."

Janet couldn't explain why she felt a sudden surge of anger towards the dark haired girl when she saw her. For three years, she wanted Kimberly to make some friends at school, and now it seemed she'd finally done just that. Janet decided not to let something she couldn't even explain ruin the first friendship her daughter had. Still, there was something familiar about the girl.

As they walked to the car and got in, Kimberly was deep in her own thoughts. 'I can't let Mom find out who Mindy really is,' she thought. 'If she had seen her mom, she would have known right away. I need to be more careful.'

Once they were home, Kimberly sat with her mother and the two of them looked over the paperwork Dr. Satish gave them. Kimberly did not know some of the terms she read, but was able to figure out their meaning from context. She seemed to have a knack for doing that, as it was how she figured out most of what she learned. Later she would look up the new words, but she would not be surprised that she guessed right. Kimberly finished reading the literature while her mother fixed a light dinner for them. Afterwards, she went up to her room and looked up the new words before starting to read her textbooks.

~*~

TWO

The next day, Janet dropped Kimberly off at school before heading back to her brother-in-law's office. She had spoken to Mike and her father-in-law, Dave, the night before, and they agreed to meet with her and her father to go over all of her financial records to see if it would be feasible to bring Krystal home. When Janet called her father, he suggested that he and her mother spend the night with her so that they could drive in together.

When Adam Greene and Janet walked into the law offices of Learner and Tucker, David and Mike Tucker were already there to meet them.

"Come on into the conference room," Mike said after giving Janet a hug. "Adam, your office sent the files over already."

"Great," Adam said, following them down the hall.

The morning was spent pouring through all of Janet's financial information and going over all of the medical options with David, a retired doctor, and legal options with Mike, the family's lawyer. They realized that without government assistance Krystal could only be cared for at home for two years before Janet ran the risk of losing custody of her and their home as well. David and Adam agreed to set up a savings account, the interest from which would cover the annual expenses for Krystal's care, but Janet would still need to return to work eventually, or risk losing her home.

~*~

Angela opened her good eye and looked around. 'Damn,' she thought as she realized she was in the hospital. She knew that Joyce had brought her last night, but she didn't remember being admitted. She raised her head to look around and saw that Joyce and the two kids were not here. Her head started to swim, so she laid back down wondering where Joyce and the kids went.

"Miss Winston?" A female voice asked.

"Huh?" Angela questioned. 'Winston?'

"My name is Regina Kane," the woman said. "I'm the charge nurse for this floor. Dr. Daniels asked me to let him know when you woke up. He'll be in here in a few minutes. I'm just going to check your vitals real quick."

"Okay," Angela said. 'Why did she call me Winston? I haven't gone by my maiden name since I got married.' While the nurse worked on checking her blood pressure and taking her temperature, Angela wondered why Joyce would check her into the hospital under her maiden name.

"Before I forget, your sister left this for you," Regina said handing an envelope to her.

After the nurse left, Angela opened the envelope and removed the note. Focusing all of her attention on the paper, the words slowly began to form clearly and she read.

Angie,

I took the kids to a motel a couple of blocks from here and ran home to get us all a change of clothes. I'm going to take them to

school in the morning and we'll be back by 3:30 to pick you up. I
checked you in under your maiden name in case asshole comes
here looking for you. If he shows up, call the police.
Love, Joyce

Angela put the note back in the envelope and started crying. In eleven years of marriage, despite his habit of talking to her like crap, Jason had never hit her. True, she had thrown a full can of beer at him, but to beat her like this...she would never have seen this coming. She was still crying when the baritone voice interrupted her thoughts.

"Miss Winston," the man greeted cautiously.

Angela opened her eye and waited for it to focus on the new visitor.

"I'm glad to see you awake," the man said as he came in and looked down at the clipboard in his hand. "You had a concussion when you were brought in. Your nose is broken and two of your ribs are seriously bruised." He looked down at her and his expression softened. "Miss Winston, your sister said that you had a very bad fall down some stairs, but I have to tell you, I have been in medicine long enough to know the difference between a fall and a beating."

Angela raised her head to protest, but was stopped by a soft hand on her shoulder. "Miss Winston," he continued. "Your sister's statement is in the record and I will not change it, but while you are here, between the two of us I insist upon honesty. I promise not to interfere in your life until and unless you ask me to, okay?" Angela nodded and the doctor continued. "Now, was it your husband that did this, or someone else?"

Fresh tears began flowing as Angela mumbled, "My husband."

"Was this the first time?"

"Yes."

"Has he been abusive in any other way?" the doctor asked. "Verbally, emotionally or sexually?"

"No," Janet said. "He cusses a lot, but nothing serious."

Doctor Daniels looked at her for a moment before continuing, "Are you afraid to go home if we release you?"

The question caught Angela off guard. She had never been afraid to go home before. She was definitely afraid now. 'Would Jason beat me like this again?' She asked herself. 'Would he have done it this time if I hadn't hit him first?' The answer to both questions was more uncertain, but the same one she gave the doctor, "No," she said with more confidence than she felt.

Eric Daniels had seen more than his share of abused women come before him for treatment, and was loathing letting another one go back into a situation where he knew, better than anyone, what the result would be. Unfortunately, his hands were legally tied.

It was with more than a few reservations that he told her, "We are going to release you this afternoon. I will give you a few phone numbers when you leave. I hope that you're right, Miss Winston, and that you never need to use them, but I am begging you to consider that spousal abuse quite often leads to other forms of abuse. If you find yourself in any danger or feel that your children are in danger please promise to call these numbers and get yourself and your children out of that house."

"It won't be a problem," she whispered. "This won't happen again."

"I pray that you're right," the doctor said. "If you come in with these kinds of injuries again, I'm afraid I will have to report them to the proper authorities for your own and your children's safety."

Angela nodded and waited for the doctor to say more. He just sat there for a few moments looking at her before standing and making a note on her chart. "Are you in any pain right now?" he asked.

"A little," she said. "My jaw and ribs are sore."

"I'll have the nurse bring you some pain killers," he said. "And I'll write you a prescription you can have filled at the pharmacy here in the hospital." Angela nodded again, and the doctor turned to leave.

A few hours later, Joyce arrived with Mindy and JJ who started crying when he saw the bruises on his mother's face. Angela's heart broke to see her little boy so scared. Within an hour, the doctor released her and she left the hospital without stopping to fill her prescriptions.

~*~

Janet and Kimberly walked into the house, both lost in their own thoughts. They both headed automatically into the kitchen,

Kimberly to do her homework at the table and Janet to start dinner. Just as Janet began slicing the vegetables for the spaghetti, Kimberly put down her pencil and watched her.

"Mom?" she began. "When Kryssi comes home, she's gonna need her own room."

"Not really," Janet said as she grabbed a pepper from the crisper.

"Think about it," Kimberly said. "She's gonna need a few machines in there and they're not exactly quiet."

"And?" Janet said.

"Well, I was thinking. The guest room is where Grandma and Grandpa sleep when they visit."

"Uh-huh," Janet said putting her knife down to pay closer attention to her daughter. "So, what, you want to put your sister in the attic?"

"No," Kimberly nearly laughed, knowing her mother was kidding. "I'm thinking she should have our room to herself."

"So you want to go to the attic?"

"Ew, no."

"Then what were you thinking?"

"Well, the front part of the basement is carpeted and Daddy was going to put up a wall to separate it from his work area."

"And you figure we could go ahead and put up that wall and you sleep in the basement?"

"Yeah," Kimberly said, proud of her idea.

"Well, there's a couple of problems with your plan," Janet said coming around the counter to sit across from her daughter. "First of all, there's the fact that neither of us know how to build a wall."

"But Uncle Bob does."

"Second," Janet said, "There's the cost. I don't know how much it would cost to build a wall, but I don't think it will be cheap." She noted Kimberly's confidence falter but continued. "And most importantly, there's the fact that you're eight years old."

"I know a lot of eight-year-olds who have their own room." Kimberly said.

"In the basement?" Janet said with a smirk.

"Well, no," Kimberly said with a small frown. "Probably not. But it's not like it's at the other end of the world."

"It's two whole floors from my bedroom," Janet said. "What if I have a nightmare? Are you going to hear me from that far away? Are you gonna run up two whole flights of stairs to come rescue me?"

In spite of herself, Kimberly giggled at her mother's argument. She knew she was defeated, so she picked up her pencil and returned to her homework, hoping a better plan came to mind. Janet smiled at her daughter before returning to her own work.

Kimberly finished her homework just as Janet began draining the pasta. After putting away her books and washing her hands, she grabbed the dishes and began setting the table. Once the spaghetti and garlic bread were on the table, Janet sat down and looked at Kimberly again, when an idea hit her.

"I've been thinking," she said. "And you're right."

"I get to move into the basement?" Kimberly asked, surprise in her voice.

"Honey, I said you were right, not that I was crazy," Janet said watching Kimberly deflate. "But Kryssi will need her own room."

"So, we're gonna use the guestroom, huh."

"Yes," Janet said, putting some spaghetti on Kimberly's plate. "For guests. I know that you want your own room to show that you're independent, but I can't have two floors separating us."

"So..." Kimberly said. "Please tell me you're not going to put me in the attic."

Janet snorted before saying, "No. We're going to turn the den into a bedroom."

"For me?"

"No," Janet said. "For Kryssi." Kimberly didn't bother to hide her disappointment. "Don't get upset. Think about it for a minute. When we bring her home it will be hard to get her upstairs, yeah?"

Kimberly pictured having people carry a hospital bed up the stairs and saw several complications right away. "Okay, yeah I can see that."

"And what if, God forbid, something happens and we need to call an ambulance? We'd have the trouble of bringing her back down the stairs and taking her back up when she came back home right?"

Kimberly nodded. "Okay," she said conceding her mother's point. "I think this would be better anyway. That way we can open the doors in the den on warm days and it would be like we were outside playing."

"See?" Janet said smiling. "That's why you skipped two grades. You're smarter than all of us."

After dinner, Janet and Kimberly started working in the den packing up the books and papers to take downstairs. Once they had all of the boxes down in the basement, they began working on storing them in the work area. Just as they were finishing, Janet noticed a box under the worktable and bent to pull it out, thinking that Kimberly must have just placed it there.

After pulling it out, she realized it had been there for a while based on the thick layer of dust on the lid. Janet wiped the dust off and her blood ran cold. Her old files on Jason McDowell had been down here the whole time. She thought her father or David had thrown it out, but they had obviously brought it down here instead. Kimberly watched as her mother lifted the lid with shaky hands.

"What are we going to do with the furniture in the den?" Kimberly asked, hoping to distract her mother.

"We'll figure something out," Janet said. She closed the lid of the box and picked it up. "I need to go through this," she said heading for the stairs. "It's time to throw this crap away."

Kimberly breathed a sigh of relief as she followed her mother upstairs. Tired from all of the work today, Kimberly went to bed early hoping that her mother really was going to throw that box out. She hoped even more that her mother wouldn't notice the missing information that she had taken out a few months earlier.

~*~

Joyce helped Angela into the house and up the stairs. She noticed out the corner of her eye that Jason was passed out on the sofa. Mindy and JJ were close behind the women as they ascended the stairs. Once Angela was in bed, Joyce took the kids downstairs to fix them some dinner. She set Mindy at the table to do her homework and gave JJ some toys to play with. By the time she was putting dinner on the table, Bill came in the back door.

"Where did you guys go last night?" he asked Joyce.

"Jason didn't tell you?"

"No, he was passed out when I got home."

"He beat the shit out of Angie and we took her to the hospital."

"What?" Billy asked in shock.

"Yeah," Joyce said. "Come here. Kids eat your dinner, we'll be right back."

Joyce led Billy upstairs and opened Angela's bedroom door. "Damn," Billy whispered, not wanting to wake his sister-in-law. The huge bruises on her face and swollen eye made his stomach knot. "Why did he do that?"

"I don't know why he does anything," Joyce answered. "She couldn't tell me what happened. Bill, I want him out."

"What?" Billy asked.

"I want him out of this house away from her and the kids."

"J, he's never done anything like this before."

"Bullshit," Joyce whispered violently. "He treats her like shit. He acts as if her sole purpose is to serve him. Now he's beat the hell out of her."

"I think it's just stress," Billy said. "He hasn't been the same since the accident."

"What accident?" Joyce snapped. "He came here that day and got loaded and drove into that man and his little girl. Everything that has happened to him is his own damned fault."

"J, he helped us when I was out of work."

"I don't care." Joyce said. "That doesn't give him the right to do this," she said, pointing to Angela's bedroom.

"Okay," Billy said. "Give me a few days to figure things out."

"I don't want any more beer in this house while he's here," Angela said.

Billy sighed, not looking forward to telling his brother that the house was going to be dry from now on. He looked at his wife, then looked at Angela's closed door. Remembering the bruised face of the woman on the other side, he nodded and turned for the stairs.

"Take the kids upstairs after supper," he said as they went through the living room. "I'm gonna have a talk with him."

"All I want is for that conversation to end with 'goodbye,'" Janet hissed.

"Just let me handle it."

~*~

Wednesday morning found Janet sitting at the kitchen table looking through the files on Jason McDowell and his family. Janet closed the last folder and set it aside. Closing her eyes, she started to cry, thinking of that day when the man whose face she had just stared at had shattered her world. Three years have gone by and still the bastard hadn't seen a moment of justice. Three years and her husband was still gone. Her daughter was still in a coma. Her life was in pieces and this bastard was living happily not even thinking about the lives he destroyed.

'Maybe it's time for him to be punished for everything he did,' Janet thought to herself. 'Maybe I'm supposed to punish him myself.' Janet took the files and tossed them back into the box. She then carried the box into the living room and sat it in front of the hearth. "I don't think I'm going to want anyone knowing I have these," she said as she opened the floo. Janet watched as each file burned to ash and then she threw the box into the fire for good measure. When the fire was at last burned out, she went upstairs to change clothes. She hadn't slept at all last night and she had a lot to do today.

Janet took Kimberly to visit Krystal for the last time. By Friday, she would have both of her daughters at home again, but before that happened she needed to take care of a few things. After dropping Kimberly off at school, Janet came home and changed clothes. Wearing a black blouse and slacks, she left the house half an hour later and drove over to Willowood Lane and parked two houses away from the address she wanted to watch.

No sooner had she turned off the ignition did she see two women exiting the house with two children. Janet broke out in a cold sweat as she recognized the brunette girl as the same one Kimberly spoke to at the hospital Monday evening. 'Oh crap,' she thought to herself. 'My daughter is friends with Jason McDowell's daughter.'

Janet watched as the women drove away, presumably taking the kids to school. She waited a bit longer and watched a man come out of the house carrying a lunchbox. 'This must be his brother,' Janet thought. 'McDowell moved in with him just before the trial.' No sooner had the black pickup left than Janet saw Jason McDowell, himself, come out of the house and get into his tan pickup. The same pickup, Janet realized, that he buried in Dugan's bakery the day he killed her husband. As McDowell backed into the street, Janet started her own engine and began following the pickup.

Jason was soon more than half a mile ahead of Janet, as he paid no heed to stop signals or speed limits. Janet did her best to keep up with him and eventually followed him to a lumberyard outside of town. As she watched him, Jason went in and spoke with first one man, then two others before shaking hands with all three and leaving. Following him home proved more difficult for Janet as he decided to drive even faster than when he left. Once she drove past the house on Willowood Lane and saw his pickup back in the driveway, she decided that it would be best to let someone else find out the information she needed.

On her way home, Janet went through the possibilities for hiring another private investigator. She couldn't use the same one as before. She didn't want to seem like a stalker. She made her way home on autopilot while she went over the different possibilities.

~*~

"So she's just been in a coma for three years?" Mindy asked.

"Yeah," Kimberly answered. "Okay, enough about my sister. How's your mom doing?"

"She's better," Mindy said. "She came home yesterday. JJ wanted to stay home with her today, but she had to go back to work."

"Alright everyone," Mrs. Estep interrupted everyone's conversations. "We're going to go out of order today." As the students gave their full attention, Mrs. Estep picked up her Social Studies manual. "This year we are going to have six major projects. Our first project will be for Social Studies. I will assign you into teams of two and I want each team to write a paper describing the importance of the topic I give you. Each team will have a different topic, so we should have plenty of great papers. Yes, Kimberly?" she acknowledged the girl as she had raised her hand.

"Do you want just a paper or should we have pictures or a model or something with it?"

"Good question," Mrs. Estep replied. "You will be graded on the paper alone, so if you want to, you can just turn that in. However, since you will be reading your papers in front of the class, I will give extra points for visual representations. You can look that word up later. I will also give extra credit for originality and presentation of your work."

Ten minutes later, much to Lesley's chagrin, Kimberly was teamed with Mindy and given the subject of elections. Lesley and her partner Kelly were given the topic of the media.

"Don't worry," Kimberly whispered to Lesley. "We can still help each other." Lesley smiled as Kimberly and Mindy put their heads together to make plans. The entire class was still keyed up with the news of their projects when they went to recess.

"Maybe I can talk my parents into letting me come over to your place this weekend to work on it," Mindy said as they headed for the door.

"I don't know," Kimberly said. "With Kryssi coming home this weekend, it might be a little crazy."

"I forgot about that," Mindy replied.

"Hold on," Kimberly said. "I think I have an idea." Kimberly left Mindy in the hallway to run back into the classroom and spoke with Mrs. Estep. Mindy watched as the teacher initially began shaking her head, denying Kimberly's request. Kimberly kept talking however and surprised her friend when the teacher said, "Huh," loud enough to be heard in the hall.

After a moment, the teacher nodded and walked with Kimberly out to the hall. "You had a good idea being friends with this one, Miss McDowell," she said as she led the girls outside.

"Okay," Kimberly said when she and Mindy met up with Lesley and Kelly on the playground. "We can't work on it at my house because my sister's coming home. Maybe we can work at one of your houses?"

"I can ask my dad," Lesley said.

Kelly said that she would ask her parents, as did Mindy.

"My house might be tricky," Mindy said. "I not only have to ask my mom and dad, but my aunt and uncle too."

"You can ask your aunt now," Lesley said.

"I'll ask her after school. She's not been feeling well lately."

The four girls sat down to talk about their projects, Kimberly going through her Social Studies book for ideas, while the other girls took notes. By the end of recess, they had a vague plan made.

~*~

Kimberly and Lesley sat on the steps of the school waiting for their parents to arrive. Mindy had already left with her mother, aunt, and brother.

"I wonder what's wrong with her," Kimberly asked.

"Who?"

"Mindy's aunt."

"Oh," Lesley said. "She's got diabetes."

"What's that?" Kimberly asked.

"It's when you have too much sugar in your body. It makes you sick and sleepy."

"How can you have too much sugar?" Kimberly asked, truly perplexed by the disease.

"I don't know," Lesley answered. "But she has to take shots every day or she gets really sick."

Kimberly was still thinking about that when her mother pulled up to the front of the school.

"Hey, sweetie," Janet said as Kimberly buckled up. "We have to hurry. They're delivering Kryssi's bed and some of her other supplies today."

Kimberly was excited to have the equipment arrive. It meant that her sister was that much closer to coming home. They left the school parking lot and Janet turned left to drive towards the hospital.

"Mom," Kimberly said.

"Yeah, baby."

"I thought we were going home."

"Shoot," Janet said, feeling silly that she had begun giving in to her usual routine. She signaled to turn at the next intersection. "So who was the girl you were just sitting with?"

"That's Lesley," Kimberly said. Suddenly a thought occurred to her. "We're working on a Social Studies project. Lesley wanted me to come over this weekend and work on it."

"I don't see why not," Janet said, "As long as her parents don't mind you coming over."

"I'll tell her to have her dad call you," Kimberly said. With that worry out of the way, Kimberly sat back in her seat and opened her science book. By the time they pulled into their driveway, she had the reading assignment finished. When Janet pulled the key from the ignition, the little girl unbuckled her belt and waited for her mother to open the back door, which for some unknown reason still had the child safety lock engaged.

They had barely made it into the house when Janet's father-in-law pulled into the drive. When he and Bob came into the house, they spent a few moments talking with Janet about what she wanted moved and where she wanted it moved to. In no time at all, they were working tirelessly while Kimberly busied herself with her homework. After she was finished, she asked her mother to use the laptop so she could look up some of the new words she'd learned today. The first word she looked up was 'diabetes'. The more the little girl read, the more fascinated she became and before long, she had a huge list of new words to look up.

The next two days went by in a blur. Mindy had secured permission from her mother, her aunt, and her uncle to host the study group for the weekend. Angela was put out of work for two weeks to give her time to heal. Joyce continued to implore Billy to kick Jason out of the house. Jason got a new job at a lumber mill and Billy hoped to put his wife off for a few more days before he had to confront his brother.

Over on Palmetto Drive, Janet and Kimberly spent Thursday evening rearranging the new furniture and medical equipment in what was now Krystal's bedroom. They decorated the room to match the girls' bedroom as much as possible, but no matter how much they tried to make it look otherwise, the room still looked like a hospital room put into a den.

"Well," Janet said, blowing a wisp of hair from her face. "With a little luck, she'll wake up and be able to move back upstairs and we can make this a den again."

"Still planning to put her in the attic?" Kimberly said straight-faced.

"No," Janet said thoughtfully. "I was up there yesterday. I found a nice corner where some squirrels had a nest and lots of spiders live. I think you'd be real happy up there." The two of them enjoyed the moment of levity before continuing to work. By the time they finished and grabbed a couple of sandwiches for dinner, it was well past bedtime.

Now the two of them stood in the living room waiting for the ambulance to arrive with Krystal. Janet wanted to go to the hospital and ride home with her daughter, but with almost all of her family either working or busy with other tasks, there would have been no one to drive her car home.

Therefore, she stood there in the living room and waited. Each car that passed the house caused her to tighten her grip on Kimberly's shoulder ever so slightly. Finally, they heard the unmistakable rattle of a diesel engine, followed by the alert claxon of a large vehicle backing up.

Janet threw the door open and held her hands to her chest. She had waited for this moment for three years. True she had always hoped that Krystal would be walking through the front door when she came home, but right now, it didn't matter if she came in walking, flying, or being carried.

Kimberly stepped aside as the paramedics brought her sister in, and her mother directed them to Kryssi's new bedroom. It took them less than twenty minutes to transfer her to the bed and set up the equipment. When they had finished and were leaving, Kimberly went into the room and sat on the end of the bed, just watching her sister lay there. Now that Kryssi was home, Kimberly decided that it was the right time to do something for her and their mother. Something she had wanted to do for three years. She leaned over and whispered into Kryssi's ear, then went out to ask her mother to use the laptop.

The first thing she did was send an email to Lesley asking if her dad could swing by and pick her up tomorrow on their way to Mindy's house. The next thing she did was look up laws involving vehicular homicide. She read about the statute of limitations and finding convictions for drunk driving when it couldn't be proven. While Kimberly was learning about the various laws and precedents, Janet called Dr. Satish to schedule his first home visit with Krystal.

~*~

Jason sat in the bar watching the baseball game. He hated the sport, but it was the only channel that the TV in this dive got, and he was stuck watching it. It irritated him that he had to be here. If Billy had any control over his woman, he could be there now enjoying his beer and watching something decent. As it was, she whipped him into making it a dry house. What was worse, she didn't 'let' Billy come to the bar with him.

'It's all that bitch's fault,' Jason thought. 'If she hadn't thrown that beer at me, I wouldn't have had to put her in her place. Maybe somebody needs to put the other smart little bitch in her place, too.' As he continued drinking, his hatred for both Joyce and Angela grew. He wanted nothing more than to go home right now and smack them both upside the head. 'Maybe knock some sense into that brother of mine too. Then take both of the bitches upstairs and show 'em how to really treat a man.'

Jason finished off his sixth beer and paid his tab. He stumbled outside to his truck and tried three times before getting his key into the door lock. Once in the truck, the heat and humidity of the night washed over him and he started feeling sick. He opened the door again and leaned out before expelling everything from his stomach onto the parking lot. Several heaves later, he spat out the remaining sour taste and sat back up in the truck. 'That ain't happened in a while,' he thought, running his fingers through his greasy hair. Getting sick didn't sober him up or change his intentions. He started the truck and put it into gear. It took him a little over five minutes to drive home, passing through red lights and other intersections along the way. Once he pulled into the drive, he stood and looked up at the house. After hitching up his pants, he bent to pick up a brick and tossed it toward the window where he knew Angela slept. If he had been sober, he might not have missed the window and hit the satellite dish instead.

Jason stomped into the house calling for his wife and sister-in-law. "You bitches get yer asses down here!" he shouted. "I'm gonna show you both how to treat a man!" Fortunately for both Joyce and Angela, they had taken the kids to get pizza tonight and weren't home for him to take out his frustrations on them. Maybe more fortunate for Jason, Billy wasn't home either, and thus did not hear his brother make such comments.

THREE

Billy kissed his wife goodbye as he grabbed his lunchbox. He stopped in the door of the kitchen and turned back to her. "Do you know what happened to the TV?" he asked her.

"No. Why?"

"I got home last night and was gonna watch the sports recap, but couldn't get a signal."

"Maybe something's wrong with the satellite," Joyce said. "I'll have Jason look at it when he comes to."

"Alright," Billy said with a sigh, knowing Jason wouldn't lift a finger for it. "I'll fix it when I get home."

Joyce smiled at her husband as he walked out. She had to admit, she liked this new, sober Billy. Now if she could just get him out from under Jason's influence completely, there was no telling how happy they could be.

Joyce looked in on her brother-in-law and went upstairs to wake the kids. Mindy's friends would be here later today to work on their school projects. She needed to figure out a way to get him out of the house before then. After waking JJ and Mindy, Joyce went into Angela's room to check on her. She was out of work for a couple of weeks, so she decided, at Joyce's insistence, to take it easy as much as possible.

Joyce felt sorry for Angela. Not only was she married to the single most deplorable man on the planet, but also the misfortune he has brought into the lives of her and their children was borderline criminal.

"The hell happened to the TV?" Jason's hung over voice bellowed from the living room. Joyce closed Angela's door quickly, hoping to keep him from waking her. She rushed downstairs and through the living room.

"The satellite's out," she said as she went into the kitchen.

"You better call and get it fixed," he shouted. "USC's playing at one and I want to watch it."

"Then you need to go somewhere else to watch it," Joyce said, coming back to the kitchen door. "Billy will fix it when he gets home… at four-thirty."

Jason grabbed the arms of the recliner, ready to jump up and put her in her place. After calming himself, he thought better of it. 'No,' he considered. 'It's time to catch a fly with honey.' Pulling his greasy hair back out of his face, he rose and made his way into the kitchen. He saw his kids sitting at the table and Joyce at the sink with her back to him. Mindy looked at him when he entered and he motioned for her to take her brother upstairs.

Without a word, Mindy took JJ's hand and quietly led him out of the kitchen. She had a feeling there was about to be a lot of yelling and she didn't want her brother to hear it. She rushed him upstairs to his room where she turned on his CD player and turned the volume up halfway. She didn't want it so loud it would wake her mother, but she also didn't want JJ to hear the swear words that were bound to come from downstairs.

Jason waited until he heard the kids heading upstairs, before going to the sink and placing a hand on each of Joyce's shoulders. Her reflexes were lightning fast. She reached her right hand out, spun, and stared her brother-in-law square in the eyes. Jason felt some pressure on his groin and looked down. Securely between his legs, with the sharp edge up, was the huge butcher's knife Joyce kept. He looked back at her with fiery hatred in his eyes.

"I have had enough of you," Joyce spat through gritted teeth. "You touch me again and I will give the most painful sex change in history."

"Get that damned knife off my dick," he growled.

"I want you out of this house now. Not in the morning, not next week, now."

"This is your last warnin'."

"Is it?" she asked. "You know, Jason, I teach for a living. Let me teach you something, now. If you hit me, you might knock me out, but then again you might not. If you don't I'm going to raise my hand and pull and you will never again be the man you used to be. If you do knock me out, there's an eighty percent chance that I'll fall backwards or to the side and the same result will happen. Even if I do fall in a way that won't cut this pathetic thing you call a dick off, the knife will cut you somewhere and trust me it is sharp enough to cut deep.

"So," she continued, flipping a strand of hair from her eyes. "You can either leave, or we can both do something that will leave me bruised and you bleeding to death."

Jason stood there listening to her, his anger growing more and more by the second. He thought about what she said. Every word made sense. No matter how he worked it out in his mind, this bitch was gonna end up cutting him real bad.

"Fine," he said at last. "I'm outta here. Now take that knife off my dick."

"How about I just lower it enough to let you walk and I escort you to the door. That way, you're not tempted to do anything stupid."

Jason was seething, but he gave her a quick nod and gulped nervously when he felt the pressure of the knife ease from his groin. Slowly, with her matching his every step, he backed to the living room where she made him stop. With her left hand, she opened the drawer to the end table next to the kitchen door and pulled out Billy's .38 caliber revolver. Clicking off the safety, she cocked the hammer and pointed it at Jason.

He could see the tips of the bullets in the cylinder and knew the gun was loaded. He raised his hands and when she motioned, he once again began backing up toward the front door. Joyce followed, keeping the pistol aimed as Jason got into his truck. She never once lowered it until the truck turned the corner two blocks down. Once inside, she locked the door and called the kids back downstairs, taking the pistol into the kitchen with her.

"Where's Daddy?" JJ asked when he and Mindy came back in.

"He went somewhere else to watch the game," Joyce answered.

"Is the TV really out?" the little boy asked.

"Yeah, baby. But I'll try to fix it when Mindy's friends get here."

"Okay."

"Don't worry," Joyce said, looking at Mindy. "There are a lot of games on today. You girls will have plenty of peace and quiet to work on your project."

Mindy smiled at her aunt and grabbed a box of cereal. "You want some?" she asked her aunt.

"Sure," Joyce answered and grabbed three bowls from the cabinet.

~*~

Kimberly helped her mom clear the dishes from the table before going in to check on Kryssi. She knew it was too much to hope for, but she desperately wanted her sister to wake as soon as possible. There was so much happening that she wanted to share with her sister. She wanted Krystal to know everything she had accomplished and everything that she planned to do.

Before long, her mother came in and joined her. "What's the name of the friend that's coming to get you?" she asked.

"Lesley," Kimberly answered. "She and her dad will be here pretty soon."

"Don't you think you should get ready?"

"Yeah," Kimberly answered, taking hold of Krystal's hand.

"Here," Janet said. Kimberly looked at her mother, who was holding out her cellphone. "Take it with you and I'll call you if anything changes." Kimberly smiled as she took her mother's phone. "Just remember," Janet said as her daughter got up to leave, "If any calls to China show up on the bill, we're gonna have a long talk."

"Mom," Kimberly said with mock horror. "You know I don't speak Chinese." The two laughed as Kimberly headed for the door. "But I am gonna learn Italian," she called from the living room.

"I don't know how to tell you this, baby," Janet whispered to Krystal, "But your sister is adopted." With a smile, she placed a hand on the child's chest and sat there just feeling her breathe.

In no time, the front doorbell rang and Janet went to answer it. On the other side was John Tucker, back from the dead and smiling at her. Janet shook her head to clear it, and saw that the man standing on her porch actually looked nothing like John. Where John was a tall man with an athletic build, this man was average height and slender. His brown hair wasn't even styled like John's blonde hair. Janet had no idea why she had seen her late husband when she opened the door, but she was far from displeased by the man's actual appearance.

"Hi," he said. "I'm Dan Bennett, Lesley's father."

"Oh, of course," Janet said, inviting him in. "Kimberly should be ready in a minute."

"I'm ready, Mom," Kimberly said as she came into the room with her backpack in hand.

To Mr. Bennett, Janet asked, "Now are you sure this is not a problem for you?"

"Not at all," he answered. "We were driving by here anyway."

"No I mean-"

"Mom," Kimberly interrupted. "We've only got a couple of hours to figure out our outline and get the parts assigned."

"I'm sorry," Janet said as she handed Mr. Bennett a slip of paper. "Mr. Bennett, this is our house number, should anything happen."

"Thank you," Mr. Bennett said. "We'll see you in a few hours."

Mr. Bennett held the car door open and pulled the front seat forward so Kimberly could climb into the back seat next to Lesley. Once he got into the car, he put it into reverse and looked back.

"Hold on," Kimberly said, sliding the belt across her lap. Once it clicked into place, she nodded at him. "Ready," she said.

"You need to take some lessons from this girl," Mr. Bennett told Lesley with a smile. The girl returned his smile with a smirk before fastening her own seatbelt and sticking her tongue out at her friend. Once they were at the street corner, he reached for the device on his dashboard. "Where on Willowood are we going?"

"452," Lesley and Kimberly said together.

Janet watched the car leave the driveway and head down the street. Once they were out of sight, she went back into the house and dialed her mother's number.

~*~

Joyce grabbed the bottle of pain medicine from the counter and dropped one in her hand. Angela didn't tell her about the prescription when they left the hospital on Tuesday. She found it amongst the discharge papers the next day and took it to be filled.

She knew Angela couldn't afford the pills on her own and Jason wouldn't give her the money if he had it, so she paid for it herself. After filling a glass of water, she went upstairs to make her sister-in-law take the pill.

Joyce had only just stepped back into the hall after making sure Angela was comfortable, when a knock came at the front door. She quietly made her way downstairs, and in the middle of the second round of knocking, opened the door to find Dan Bennett and two girls standing on her porch.

"Mrs. McDowell," Dan said. "I understand you're hosting this study group?"

Joyce smiled and stepped back to allow the three of them to enter. "It's actually Mindy hosting it," she said. "I'm just providing snacks and advice."

Dan Bennett handed his daughter her book bag and said, "I have to be honest, I was suspicious when Lesley said they would be studying."

"I know," Joyce said. "I was surprised, too. But I understand this young lady here is responsible for getting them to study," she gestured to Kimberley.

Kimberly tried to brush off the compliment. She was more intensely aware of where she was now. Before this moment, her plans for the day were abstract. She never considered how she would feel actually being inside the house of Jason McDowell. She thought about her father that morning asking her and Krystal if they wanted to go get their mother's cake. She thought about the coffin that they weren't allowed to open at his funeral. She thought about her sister lying in the hospital for over three years. All of these thoughts burned through her eight-year-old mind and she could barely control herself enough to be excused to join Mindy and Lesley in the kitchen.

Dan Bennett left the McDowell house after speaking with Joyce for a few minutes and promising to return to pick up Lesley and Kimberly in a few hours, or when she called to tell him they were ready.

A few minutes later, Janet's blue Taurus pulled to the curb across from the McDowell house. Janet noted that Jason's pickup was gone, but an old Buick Delta 88 sat in the drive. She decided to sit and wait to see when Jason came home. She wanted to learn his pattern and maybe catch him driving drunk or something that she could report and finally have him put in jail for. 'Or better yet,' she thought, 'Watch him die, like John.'

Inside the house, Kimberly was starting to relax. Mindy had told her that her dad had gone somewhere else to watch football so they could work without any distractions. Mindy didn't tell her friends how relieved she was that her dad wasn't home. Mindy had always loved her dad despite the way he acted towards her mom. That is to say, she loved him until the end of the school year last year. She had overheard her mother and aunt talking about her dad killing a man. Mindy figured that was the reason they had to move in with Uncle Billy and Aunt Joyce.

No one ever explained the situation to her, so since she learned about what he did, she began looking at him differently. She no longer saw the superhero that could do anything. Now she saw the lazy drunk who was verbally abusive to her mother. She suspected that her mother's injuries came from her father and not a fall down the stairs as she and Aunt Joyce said.

She decided to worry about her dad and his problems later. For now, she had her best friend and her new friend here ready to work. She looked at the clock on the wall and figured she'd give Kelly a little more time before calling to see if she was coming. Lesley and Kimberly were going over ideas for Lesley's part of the assignment.

"Okay, girls," Joyce said, coming into the kitchen. "Help yourselves to anything you want to drink. I need to go fix the satellite so JJ can watch TV and stay out of your hair."

"Thank you, Mrs. McDowell," Kimberly said and went back to helping Lesley write out an outline.

Joyce climbed the stairs and peeped into Angela's room to check on her. Seeing her sister-in-law still asleep, she proceeded to her bedroom and turned the TV on and the volume up. The satellite dish was just outside her bedroom window at the front of the house. All she had to do was to climb out and make adjustments until she heard the TV station come through instead of static white noise. She gingerly made her way out the window and onto the hot roof. 'I really should have put on some shoes to do this,' she thought as she crouched to grab the dish.

Janet looked up from her notepad and saw the woman crouching on the roof of the house. 'Crap,' she thought. 'When did she come out here?' She turned the key and hit the button to raise the window.

~*~

Joyce saw the glare come up suddenly from the corner of her vision and looked up. The glare was coming from what looked like a blue Ford parked across the street. She looked to see if she could recognize the car, when suddenly the satellite dish came loose from the roof and threw her off balance. She tried standing to keep her balance, but overcorrected and tipped forward. She stepped forward to keep he balance and managed to stay on her feet.

Her heart beating fast, Joyce looked at the dish in her hand with dismay. 'Well,' she thought. 'I guess now I have to call someone.' She didn't see the nail lying on the shingle until she stepped on it. When she felt the tip sink into her flesh, she jerked her foot up. Too late, she realized her mistake as she tipped over the edge of the roof and plunged toward the driveway below.

~*~

Janet watched in horror as the woman fell from the roof and landed violently on the hood of the Buick, shattering the windshield. Her first instinct was to run over and check on her, but she quickly considered the repercussions if anyone were to learn of her connection to these people. She looked up and down the street and saw no one else. Without further hesitation, she started her car and put it in gear. She drove as quickly as she dared out of the neighborhood. Occasionally she would check her rearview mirror to see if anyone was following her or if the police were somehow alerted to her presence at the scene.

Janet's heart was still hammering in her chest as she pulled into her own driveway five minutes later. She got out of her car and practically ran inside, closing and locking the door behind her. 'Oh my 'God,' she thought once she made it to the kitchen. 'She looked right at me. Did I cause her to fall?'

"Yes," her mother said, coming into the kitchen.

"What?" Janet asked in confusion, turning around in surprise.

"I understand, doctor," Jean Greene said, switching the phone to her other ear. "Janet is here now and I'll let her know. Yes, thank you."

"Who- uhm, wha- wh-who was that?" Janet asked, trying to get her nerves under control.

"That was Dr. Satish," her mother replied. "He said to tell you that he will be coming by to check in on Krystal tomorrow."

"Oh," Janet said, turning to the sink. After filling a glass with water and downing it immediately, she felt her mother's hand on her shoulder.

"Are you okay," Jean asked, feeling her daughter stiffen at her touch.

"Y- yeah," Janet answered shakily. "It's just-," she thought quickly. "I- someone cut me off a few minutes ago. It- it sort of shook me up a little."

"I can imagine," her mother said sympathetically.

Janet took a shaky breath and set her glass in the sink. "Did Kimberly or Mr. Bennett call while I was out?"

"No," Jean said. "It's been quiet, except for Dr. Satish's call."

"Good," Janet said as the two went into the living room.

~*~

Kelly Winston pedaled her bicycle along the sidewalk, being careful to avoid the larger cracks and holes where pieces of concrete were missing. She saw Mindy's house just ahead. It looked like someone was lying on Mrs. McDowell's car. Kelly pushed her bike into the McDowell's yard and laid it down, grabbing her backpack from the handlebars. She looked over at the car and saw it was a woman lying on it, but something seemed wrong to her.

She walked over to the car and saw Mrs. McDowell with blood running from her and down the hood, her head at an unnatural angle. Kelly knew intuitively that her former teacher was dead and the horror of that fact welled up in her and escaped through her lips in a high-pitched shriek of terror.

Mindy and Kimberly listened as Lesley began reciting five benefits of the media in U.S. society. Just as the girl got to number four, all three of them jumped at the sound of a loud scream coming from outside.

Together, the three of them ran to the front door and out onto the porch. Kimberly saw them first and ran towards the driveway where Kelly stood screaming. She saw Joyce McDowell lying on the hood of her Buick; blood running down the hood and front fender. She put her hand in front of the woman's nose and mouth, but felt nothing.

"Call 9-1-1," she shouted, turning back to the girls on the porch. Neither of them moved, they were so transfixed on the scene before them. Kimberly grabbed Kelly by the arm and dragged her to the porch, then hustled all three girls inside. Once she got them in and closed the door, she ran to the kitchen to pull her mother's cell phone from her bag. She called for an ambulance then ran back outside to wait for them. In a few minutes, the front door opened and Mindy's mother walked out of the house.

"Sweetheart," she called through clenched teeth. "Come inside, you don't need to see this." Kimberly went back up the steps and took Angela's hand.

"It's okay Mrs. McDowell," she said. "The ambulance is on its way, but you need to sit down."

Angela ignored the child and went down the steps and over to her sister-in-law. She didn't need to be a doctor to see that the woman's neck was broken. She heard sirens approach as tears began falling down her face. In no time, an ambulance and two police cars were stopped in the street in front of the house.

~*~

While paramedics worked to get Joyce off the car, the police officers began questioning first Angela then the girls. The four officers spoke to the girls separately, presumably to get this unpleasantness over with quickly. The officer who spoke with Kimberly introduced himself as Officer Morrow and sat with her in the kitchen.

"Mrs. McDowell says that you're the one who found your teacher," he said after asking her if she wanted anything to drink.

"No," Kimberly said. "Kelly found her. We were in here working on a school project when we heard her scream. It's just when we went outside they were scared and didn't know what to do, so I brought them back inside and called 9-1-1."

"That was a very smart thing to do," Officer Morrow said. "And then what did you do?"

"I didn't know how bad she was hurt, so I went back outside to see. I couldn't feel her breathe when I put my hand in front of her, but I stayed there and let her know someone was coming."

"Did you let the other Mrs. McDowell know what happened?" he asked. Kimberly shook her head no. "Why not?"

"Mindy's mom got hurt the other day," Kimberly said. "I knew she wasn't feeling well, but I didn't know she was home, and…"

"And what?"

"And I didn't think to check to see if anyone else was home," Kimberly said, lowering her head. "I just knew I wanted to be there for Mrs. McDowell."

"That's very brave and kind of you," Officer Morrow said. "Now, why don't we call your mom and dad and have one of them come pick you up?"

"My daddy's dead," Kimberly said.

Officer Morrow blinked several times, slightly surprised. The information of her father's death didn't bother him. It was the calm, matter-of-fact manner that she had said it, which gave him pause. "Well, your mom then," Officer Morrow said after he got over his surprise.

"I have her cell phone," she said. "She gave it to me in case I needed to call Mr. Bennett to come bring me home early."

"Who is Mr. Bennett?"

"Lesley's dad," she said pointing through the kitchen door to her friend.

"Okay," he said standing up. "Hold on just a minute." Officer Morrow went into the living room to talk to the officer interviewing Lesley. After receiving a nod from the other officer, he came back into the kitchen.

"It looks like Mr. Bennett is just going to take his daughter home," he said. "Why don't you get your stuff together and I'll run you home real quick."

Kimberly started to panic. 'What if he tells Mommy what happened?' she thought. 'He'll tell her where I was. Maybe I can call... No, Grandma will tell her, too.' She never planned for this. Her mother couldn't find out where she was today. It would upset her too much. She needed time to think.

"Can I use the bathroom real quick?" she asked as she got to her feet.

"Sure," he said and led her into the living room where Mrs. McDowell sat consoling Mindy and crying herself.

"Mrs. McDowell," he said. "Can she use your bathroom real quick?"

Angela nodded and looked at the girl. She really recognized the child for the first time and a chill ran down her spine. "U-upstairs," she stuttered in shock. "Se- second door on the right." She watched as Kimberly went upstairs, and then turned to Mindy. "How do you know the Tucker girl?" she asked.

"She's in my class," Mindy answered.

"She can't be," Angela said. "She's got to be at least two years younger than you."

"She skipped a couple of grades," Mindy said.

"You didn't know Miss Tucker was here?" Officer Morrow asked.

"No, I-" Angela began, and then took a deep breath. "I was upstairs resting. I had an accident a couple of days ago and Joyce was taking care of the kids for me."

"But you do know her," he said.

"I know who she is," Angela said. "Her father-" she stopped there and looked at her daughter. "Her father died a couple of years ago."

Officer Morrow nodded and walked over to speak with his partner again.

~*~

Kimberly entered the bathroom and closed the door. Her breath came out in short, panicked gasps as she looked around for some way out of this mess. There was no window in the bathroom, so she couldn't sneak out and try to walk home. Besides, her backpack was still downstairs. 'Maybe I can distract him on the way home and he'll forget to tell Mommy why he brought me instead of Mr. Bennett,' she thought. 'No. She'll eventually ask him.' She looked around the bathroom and saw some medicine on the shelf beside the sink. Looking closely, she saw a couple of glass bottles with some milky liquid in them. Beside the bottles were a handful of needles.

She examined the other bottles but most of them were different over-the-counter medicines. Finally, after a few minutes, she realized there was no way out of her situation. She flushed the toilet and waited a moment before leaving the bathroom and returning downstairs. After retrieving her backpack, she came back to the living room and hugged Mindy before leaving with the police officer. Kimberly did not see Angela watching her as she left.

~*~

Janet took another sip of her tea before setting it on the coffee table. Her mother was still trying to calm her nerves, but all she could think about was that woman looking at her just before falling from the roof. 'What if she recognized me?' Janet thought. 'What if she tells the police I was there and that I distracted her? Did I make her fall?' Janet was starting to worry herself into a panic attack, when the doorbell rang.

Janet gave a small squeal and her mother laid a hand on her arm. "It's probably Kimmy," Jean said. "I don't imagine she has a key."

"No," Janet said getting up somewhat relieved. "I think she's too young for one right now."

"Maybe," Jean said picking up the teacups and taking them into the kitchen. Janet meanwhile opened the door and saw a police officer on the other side.

"Mrs. Tucker?" the officer asked. Janet responded by fainting on the spot.

~*~

Billy McDowell crashed through the doors of the emergency room and ran to the admittance desk. "My wife was just brought in," he said quickly. "They said she fell off the roof."

"What is her name, sir?" the woman behind the desk asked.

"Joyce," he said wiping a line of sweat from his forehead. "Joyce McDowell."

The woman typed the name into the computer and a dark look came over her. "Mr. McDowell," she said getting up. "If you'll come with me, the doctor will be with you in a moment."

Billy followed the woman through a set of doors and down a hallway to a waiting area. She showed him to a seat and asked if he needed anything before telling him that the doctor would be right with him.

The wait was torture for Billy. He was more anxious tonight than he was the day of his brother's accident, when he was rushed into surgery. He kept looking at the clock, but it seemed like the hands weren't moving. It seemed like they only moved one tick every twenty minutes. Just as Billy was about to burst, a doctor came down the hallway and sat beside him.

"Mr. McDowell," the doctor began. "Your wife suffered a very traumatic fall in which the second, third, and fourth cervical vertebrae were shattered. There were also some lacerations to her head, neck, and back as well as catastrophic contusions to her skull."

"Well, wait," Billy said, his voice beginning to shake. "Do-does this mean she's gonna be paralyzed? Or is she gonna need surgery or what?"

The doctor looked at him with a sad expression. "Mr. McDowell," he said. "Your wife arrived here in arrest. We did everything we could, but we couldn't revive her."

"What do you mean? Are-" Billy paused as anguish overtook him. "Are you sayin'…? What is it you're sayin'?"

"I'm sorry, Mr. McDowell," the doctor said as he rose to his feet.

"No," Billy cried. "No, you don't be sorry. You do somethin'!" his shouts were becoming louder as his torment increased. "You go in there and do somethin' for her! Don't tell me you're sorry!"

"Mr. McDowell," the doctor said. "Is there someone we can call for you?"

"I want you to call whoever you need to, to help my wife!" Billy cried out. "I swear, doctor, don't worry about what it's gonna cost. I swear I'll pay you every cent. Just please, please go help her." By the time he finished his sentence, Billy McDowell was on his knees before the doctor, clinging to his lab coat for dear life. As his tears hit the carpeted floor of the waiting room, he bowed his head sobbing and begging the doctor to do something.

This was how Jason found his brother two minutes later. The doctor had a hand on the top of Billy's head trying to comfort the man. Jason rolled his eyes and shook his head. He walked over to his brother and shoved the doctor out of the way. As he pulled his brother to his feet, he tried shaking him to get his attention.

"Hey," he said as his brother continued to cry. "Hey! Stop it! Get ahold of yerself." Jason smacked his brother's face trying to get his attention.

"Jason, stop it," Angela said coming around the corner.

"Why ain't you out there with the kids?" he asked.

"Mindy is watching JJ," Angela said. "I figured Billy would need some help."

"I got Billy," Jason said. "We're on our way now."

"I hate to interrupt," the doctor said. "But Mr. McDowell needs to fill out some paperwork."

"Do it yerself," Jason said. "I'm takin' him home."

"Jason, for God's sake," Angela said stepping up to Billy. "Billy," she said. "I need you to listen to me." Billy looked up at his sister-in-law. The agony on his face nearly ripped her heart in two, but she needed to handle the tasks he wasn't ready for yet.

"Billy," she said grabbing his arm. "The hospital needs someone to fill out the paperwork and get everything squared away." Billy nodded. "Do you want me to handle that for you?" Again, he nodded. "Alright," she said. "You go home with Jason and the kids. I'll handle this and drive your truck home." Billy nodded again before allowing his brother to half lead, half drag him away. Angela turned to the doctor with a small smile.

"Thank you for not saying anything, Dr. Daniels," she said.

"Thank you for not coming in here with more bruises," he replied with a smile. "If I'm not much mistaken, the gruff 'gentleman' must have been your husband."

"Yes," she said. "Billy is my brother-in-law."

"And his wife is your sister?"

"No," Angela said. "She just told the hospital that so she could check me in and make sure I was taken care of."

"I see," Dr. Daniels said with a nod. "I really hate to ask this, but did Mr. McDowell…"

Angela looked at him for a moment before she understood what he meant. "No!" she exclaimed. "Oh, no. Billy was at work when this happened. No, doctor, Billy is nothing like his brother. He would rather cut his own arm off than to hurt Joyce." The analogy, though apt, reminded Angela of why she was there and tears began sliding down her face all over again.

"Come with me," the doctor said. "We'll get everything taken care of as quickly as we can." As he led her through the emergency department, Angela thought back to just a few days ago when Joyce had brought her here. It wasn't fair that they wouldn't again be leaving this place together, as they did then.

~*~

FOUR

"Mrs. Tucker," the voice said. "Mrs. Tucker, are you alright?"

"You have to forgive her, officer," the voice of Jean Greene said. "The last time the police came to the house was when her husband was killed and her daughter put into a coma."

"Yes, ma'am," the other voice said. "We have an ambulance on the way."

"What?" Janet moaned as she opened her eyes. "What happened?"

"Mrs. Tucker," the officer said. "Can you tell me where you are?"

"I'm at home," Janet answered. "What is going on?"

"You passed out, ma'am," he said.

"Why," Janet began and then focused on the man speaking. "How did you know to come here?" She was convinced that he was here to arrest her for fleeing the scene of the accident earlier.

"There was an accident at your daughter's friend's house," the officer said, helping Janet to her feet and then to the sofa. "Mr. Bennett took his daughter home, so I offered to bring your daughter home. She gave me the address."

"Th- Thank you," Janet stammered. As her mind cleared and her pulse returned to normal, it occurred to her that a police officer had brought Kimberly home and he was now kneeling at her side, trying to check her pulse. "Why? What happened? There was an accident?"

"Yes, ma'am," Officer Morrow answered as he rose to his feet. "Hold on for a second." He grabbed the microphone from his shoulder and spoke, "Three-oh-eight to Central."

"Central," the voice from his radio responded. "I need a '10-22', disregard on the '10-52'. Subject is conscious and alert."

"Ten-four 308," the voice responded. "I have sent a disregard for the 10-18. EMS is still en-route, however."

"Ten-four," the officer said before returning his attention to Janet. "Mrs. Tucker, I called for an ambulance when you passed out. They're still going to come by to make sure you didn't hurt your head or anything when you landed on the floor."

"Where's my daughter?" Janet asked looking around.

"I sent her into Kryssi's room," Jean said. "She was starting to worry and I didn't want her upset."

"But you said there was an accident," Janet said looking back at the officer.

"Yes, ma'am," Officer Morrow said. "While your daughter was at her friend's house, the other little girl's aunt died."

"Oh my god," Janet said. "Are the girl and her father okay?"

"They're fine, ma'am," Officer Morrow assured her. "In fact, your daughter was a big help when the accident occurred. She was the only one present with the presence of mind to call 9-1-1."

"She's always been like that," Jean said. "Our Kimmy is so bright. Did you know she has already skipped two grades?"

Officer Morrow quirked an eyebrow at the older woman and

then turned towards the door as a knock interrupted the conversation and the officer asked if he could answer it. He opened the door to three paramedics. They came in and he directed them to Janet.

After a thorough examination, they determined that she had suffered a shock, but that there was no cause for alarm. Fifteen minutes after their arrival, they left with the police officer following soon after.

"Oh and ma'am," he said as he stepped out the door. "I know your daughter seems fine and calm for now, but if everything that happened today starts to bother her, feel free to call the department and ask for me. I'll be happy to come around and talk to her any time."

"Thank you," Janet said. After seeing him out and closing the door, Janet turned back to her mother. "That was the second scariest thing to happen to me today."

"Well look on the bright side, dear," Jean said. "The day is almost over. Kimmy!" the older woman called out for her granddaughter. When the girl came in to the living room, her grandmother embraced her. "Oh Kimmy," she said. "That nice policeman said you were so brave today."

"Kimberly," the little girl mumbled.

"What's that, dear?"

"Nothing," Kimberly said.

Janet and her mother immediately began questioning Kimberly about what had happened. Kimberly answered all of their questions while her mother began preparing dinner, carefully leaving out the part about her actual whereabouts, until…

"So a car just pulled into the driveway and hit her?" her grandmother asked.

"No," Kimberly answered. "She just fell on it from the roof while she was fixing the satellite." Janet dropped the pot of water she had just filled, causing her mother and daughter to jump and look over at her.

"Darn slippery handle," she said as she picked up the pot. "Mother, can you grab me the mop?" As the older woman stepped into the utility room, Janet looked at her daughter. "I think we've bothered you enough about this tonight, baby," she said. "But I do want to talk some more about it tomorrow."

Janet took the mop from her mother and cleaned up her mess, all the while trying to decide whether to be angry that her daughter misled her about where she was going, or that the girl's friend was the daughter of her father's killer. This quandary preyed on Janet's mind until bedtime and ultimately through a sleepless night.

While Janet, Jean, and Kimberly were eating a late dinner, Angela entered the house on Willowood Drive to find the kids already in bed, and Jason and Billy in the living room. She was not surprised to find Jason drinking a beer and watching TV while Billy sat on the sofa with his head in his hands. Angela went over to her brother-in-law and placed a hand on his shoulder.

"Billy," she whispered. "All of the paperwork's taken care of for the hospital. They said we can go make arrangements tomorrow." Billy began sobbing harder, eliciting a glowering stare from his brother. "I called Schaefer's Funeral Home. Someone will meet you there tomorrow afternoon. Do you want me to help you with that?" she continued. Billy nodded letting his hair drop down over his hands. His sobbing continued, and Angela pulled him into a hug, trying to comfort him.

"Get me and him a beer," Jason growled from the recliner.

"You don't need to be drinking right now," Angela said.

"You sure 'bout that?" he growled again, getting Angela's attention. As she walked into the kitchen, he said to his brother, "All you need is a couple of beers and you'll be okay."

Billy looked up at Jason and for the first time in his life, he saw what everyone else had been talking about. "I don't want any beer," he said.

"You need somethin'," Jason said. "Over there cryin' like a damned woman."

"My wife just died!" Billy exclaimed.

"And there's a million more out there," Jason said as he finished off his beer.

"Jason, stop," Angela said as she handed him his beer.

"Yeah," Billy concurred. "Just stop."

"Stop what?" Jason asked.

"Stop with the smart assed comments," Billy said as he got to his feet. "Stop with the goddamned drinkin'," he said slapping the beer from his brother's hand. "And stop all the rest of your bullshit!" the last part he shouted.

Jason jumped from the chair and locked glares with his brother. "You don't want to fuck with me," he growled to his brother.

"You're right," Billy said. "Nobody does." Jason cocked his head to the side, not understanding. "Everybody's tired of fuckin' with you. We're tired of you layin' drunk. That's why we told you no more beer in the house. We're tired of you treatin' yer wife like shit. That's why Joyce wanted me to put your ass out. And, I'm tired of makin' excuses for you. That's why I'm puttin' yer ass out."

"You're puttin' me out?" Jason asked as Angela looked on in horror. "I am your brother and you're puttin' me out?"

"Yeah," Billy said. "You're my brother. That's why I'm givin' you a week to find some place to be. Cause come next weekend, you won't be here." As he turned for the stairs, he noticed Angela standing there with a stricken look on her face. He saw the bruises still fresh on her face and his eyes softened. "Ang, you and the kids have a home here as long as you want and any time you want."

Jason and Angela watched Billy stalk up the stairs. When they heard his door close, Jason turned to his wife. "The hell was that all about?" he asked.

~*~

The sunlight broke through Kimberly's dreams and brought her into the waking world. Kimberly raised her head wondering why her curtains were opened, when she saw her mother standing by her window.

"Mom?" she said as she rubbed her eyes. "What's going on?"

Janet answered by handing Kimberly a section of the Sunday paper. The top of the page read "Police Blotter" and Kimberly scanned the notices until she saw what her mother had obviously noted. 'Uh-oh,' she thought.

"Kimberly," her mother began. "There's something I need to tell you about your friend Mindy."

'Crap,' Kimberly thought. Aloud she said, "I already know."

"Know what?" Janet asked, perplexed.

"I know who her dad is," Kimberly said.

Janet looked at her daughter in shock. It was true that Kimberly was smarter than other children were at her age, even her grade level, but it was difficult to believe that the child was smart enough to know this and have kept it hidden for so long. When she realized her mouth was hanging open, she closed it quickly and shook her head. "Oh," she said, still trying to wrap her mind around what she had just heard. "Um, how- how long have you known?"

"About three years," the little girl answered.

"Honey," Janet said, completely forgetting her carefully prepared speech. "Honey, I am so happy that you're finally making friends. But I just don't think this girl is the kind of friend you need." Kimberly drew her knees up to her chin and wrapped her arms around her legs. "I mean, I know it's not Mindy's fault what her father did, but with her as a friend, you're bound to spend some time with that…"

"Mom," Kimberly interrupted. "Don't worry. We're not going

to be friends for long."

"What do you mean?"

"I mean, next year I'll probably be in seventh grade and won't see her again."

"Well yes, there's that," Janet said. "But I'm worried about this year."

"Mom," Kimberly said. "I knew the first day that I'd be spending the entire year in class with her. I can't help that, and we're probably going to be partnered up for a few projects together. If I'm going to get through this without causing any friction, I have to smile and be friends or try to go through another school year with no one to talk to."

"I understand, baby," Janet said lowering and shaking her head. "I really do, but-"

"Mom," Kimberly interrupted again. "Relax. It won't be long before that entire family is out of our lives forever."

Janet looked at her daughter with complete wonderment, not for the first time, and smiled. "I truly wish I were as strong as you," she said. "Just promise me that you won't go back to that house."

"Mom, no offense, but if she and I have any more projects together it would be easier for me to put up with him for a few hours than for you to be around her."

Janet knew her daughter didn't mean to shame her, but she hung her head nonetheless, realizing how right her daughter was. 'If I could find some way to keep them away from us permanently, it wouldn't matter,' she thought.

After a light breakfast, Janet set about cleaning house while Kimberly took her books into Krystal's room so she could be by her sister's side while she studied. After reading her science book for the second time, she decided to give her mind a rest and scanned her father's bookshelves that her mother had left in the room. She found one particularly old book that caught her attention. She pulled the William March novel from the shelf and went over to her sister's bed, where she then sat on the end. She looked at her sister and decided to share a secret with her.

"Kryssi," she whispered. "I've got something to tell you." She traced her finger across her twin's forehead and moved a lock of her hair. "It's about the man who did this to you. His brother's wife died yesterday." Kimberly was so focused on telling Krystal this news that she missed her sister's lip twitch. "I was there when it happened." She leaned in and kissed her sister's forehead. "All I could think about was that I wished it had been him."

This time Kimberly saw the motion. As sure as she sat there on Kryssi's bed, the other child's lip twitched. "Kryssi?" she said. "Are you waking up?" No response. "Can you hear me?" Still, she saw nothing from her sister. "Did you hear what I said about that man's sister-in-law?" Again, Krystal's lip twitched.

Kimberly's heart began to pound. "Do you wish he had died too?" she whispered. She was rewarded with another twitch. "Are you going to wake up?" and just like that she stopped getting responses.

Kimberly's first instinct was to run and tell her mother, but if

Krystal didn't respond, she would have to tell her mother what was going on when she'd gotten the response. Kimberly Tucker is an exceptionally intelligent girl. She was intelligent enough to know that she did not want her mother knowing what she was saying to her sister or how badly she wanted someone dead.

Kimberly didn't realize how badly her mother wanted the same thing. In fact, as she was vacuuming the upstairs hallway, that very thought was bouncing around her mind. 'What I would have given for that to have been Jason McDowell on that roof yesterday,' she thought. 'If I had seen him fall and break his neck, I wouldn't have driven off. I would have ran over and danced on his dead chest.' The thought consumed her so much that she didn't realize she had vacuumed the same spot for ten minutes. Never in her life would she have considered wanting a man dead. Then again, never before had a man taken so much from her. The more she thought on the subject, the more she fantasized about how he should die. She imagined him being hit by a truck like his own, then a semi, and even a train before it occurred to her that the odds of those accidents occurring were too slim.

Soon, she was putting the vacuum away and fantasizing about someone actually killing him. She imagined a dark assassin stabbing him in the back, shooting him in the head or poisoning his food. 'I wonder how hard it would be to kill him,' she mused as she went downstairs to start lunch.

She peeked into Krystal's room to check on the girls, and found Kimberly sitting on the bed reading to her sister. Janet smiled at the girls and made her way into the kitchen. As she got out the stuff to make grilled cheese sandwiches and tomato soup, she thought again about the different ways Jason McDowell could die. The dark thoughts she had for the man put a strange smile on her face that stayed there until she called Kimberly to the table.

"What's got you so happy?" Kimberly asked her as she took her seat.

"You and your sister together again," Janet said after a quick thought. Then remembering seeing Kimberly reading to her sister, she smiled again, this time fueled by happy thoughts. Janet joined her daughter at the table and resolved to find a way to get Jason McDowell out of their lives, and her family on their way to healing.

~*~

Jason woke from a troubled sleep. He glanced around the living room and saw movement through the kitchen door. Staggering, he got to his feet and stumbled into the kitchen to find Angela and the kids eating breakfast. Then again, for all he knew, it might have been lunch. He made his way to the refrigerator and looked in.

"What happened to the beer?" he asked.

"Billy poured them down the sink and threw away the bottles," Angela answered.

Jason slammed the refrigerator door closed, went back into the living room, and grabbed his boots.

"Jason," Angela said following him into the living room. "Can you please not do this today? Your brother's wife just died."

"That ain't got nothin' to do with me," he said.

"I need you to watch the kids so we can go make arrangements for the funeral."

"Take 'em with you," he said as he stood up and grabbed his keys. "They might learn somethin' useful."

"You could at least take a shower."

"Jesus. Let me get woke up before you start runnin' your mouth," he snapped at her and then stalked out of the house.

"If he brings any more beer in this house I'm gonna beat his ass and put him out tonight," Billy said from the foot of the stairs.

"I don't know what I'm gonna do, Billy," Angela said as she turned back to the kitchen. "He's never been this bad before."

"Maybe he has," Billy said as he followed her. "We just ain't seen it clear till now."

"Come on, JJ," Mindy said. "Let's go get dressed."

Angela watched her children as they went upstairs, and turned to her brother-in-law. "Maybe you're right," she said. "No child her age should have to be more mature and intuitive than her parents."

"I always said kids pick up on a lot of stuff we miss."

"That's why she was such a great teacher," Angela said. "She knew kids better than any of us."

She watched Billy as he stared out the window with new tears falling down his face. She placed a hand on his shoulder and he broke down again. She gently rubbed his back as he stood there sobbing, his tears falling into the sink.

"What am I gonna to do without her?" he cried.

"I don't know," she said. "But we will get through this together. Why don't you go ahead and get dressed. We'll head over to Schaefer's."

Angela and Billy spent the afternoon at the funeral home making the necessary arrangements for Joyce's services. Based on the money Billy could spend and the payments he would have to make, they would have to have her cremated. They arranged for the services to be conducted on Tuesday and the director offered to bring her ashes to Billy by Friday. By four o'clock, the arrangements were made and the four of them left the funeral home quietly.

Angela asked Billy to stop by her job so she could pick up her paycheck and grab some groceries for dinner. Billy responded by telling her he'd grab some pizzas or something on the way home so she wouldn't have to cook tonight. The truth was, he really just wanted to get home so he could forget about everything he did today and why it had to be done. He had a nice bottle of bourbon that should do that job nicely.

When they finally pulled into the driveway on Willowood Drive, Angela and Billy both took a sharp intake of breath. Through the open window, they could see Jason inside throwing things across the room. His curses could be heard clearly from outside as could the crashes of objects hitting the walls.

"You and the kids stay here a minute," Billy said as he opened his door. He handed Angela his wallet and leaned back in saying,

"If I can't calm him down, y'all go get a room tonight." Angela started to protest, but Billy had already closed the truck door and headed inside.

~*~

She looked over her shoulder to make sure no one was watching her, and typed the words she wanted in the website's search form. Thinking about wanting a man dead earlier gave her such a thrill, she wanted to know how hard it would actually be to kill someone. She searched for hours reading stories about women who had murdered and been suspected of murder.

She read several different methods of killing and making it look like an accident. She even found a couple of articles where people had been killed and innocent people were so thoroughly framed that the real killers were never suspected until years later. She downloaded several eBooks about fictitious murders and real ones. Three hours into her research, she was interrupted by the doorbell.

~*~

Doctor Amir Satish smiled as he entered the Tucker house. "Mrs. Tucker," he said. "I hope everyone is adjusting well."

"Yes," Janet said as she closed the door. "Krystal is already getting some color back in her cheeks."

"What about you and Kimberly?" the doctor asked. "How are the two of you adapting to having to take a more active role in her care?"

"I have to say I'm a bit peeved," Janet said. When Dr. Satish gave her a worried look, she went on, "Well, according to the nurse that came when we brought her home, we have to track her vitals, which are recorded on the machines, make sure she gets 'fed' at the proper times, and reposition her periodically to prevent bed sores."

"Yes," Dr. Satish said. "And of course there's the physical therapy."

"Yes her range of motion exercises," Janet said. "They showed us that as well. In addition, of course, we're watching for any signs of her coming out of the coma, or her if condition worsening. As far as I can tell, that's basically what the hospital has done for the past three years and what a nursing home would do for her."

"Essentially, yes."

"Then why did it take so long for us to bring her home?" Janet asked. "Why could we not have brought her home two years ago, or last year?"

"To be honest," Dr. Satish said. "That was my doing." Before Janet could comment, he continued quickly, "So few family members are competent enough to perform these simple tasks at home, and fewer still are the number willing to do it." He held up a hand, halting her protest as he continued. "I'm not saying that I thought you were unable or unwilling to do it, but in my experience, it has always been best to err on the side of caution in the interest of the patient."

Janet sighed in exasperation before nodding her head. "I suppose I understand," she said. "But so much drama could have been avoided if we had known we could bring her home earlier."

"Yes," Dr. Satish said. "But now that she is home…"

"It's almost like a dream come true," Janet said. "Kimberly is almost always in there with her, either doing her homework or reading to her. She has helped with her exercises, and we take turns feeding her."

"Eight years old and taking on that much responsibility," Dr. Satish commented.

"Sometimes I think that child was a full grown adult before she was even out of diapers." Dr. Satish chuckled as Janet led him into the kitchen for some coffee. "Speaking of Kimberly," Janet said. "There was an incident yesterday."

"With Krystal?" he asked.

"No," Janet shook her head. "She was at a classmate's house yesterday and the girl's aunt fell from her roof and died."

"Oh dear," Dr. Satish said. "Did Kimberly witness the incident?"

"No, thank God," Janet said as she sat the coffee on the bar in front of the doctor. "But she did see the body. In fact, the officer who brought her home said that she called 9-1-1 and stayed with the woman until help arrived."

"Impressive," the doctor said. "Most children, even the ones as intelligent as Kimberly, would have panicked."

"I suppose," Janet said as she took a sip of her coffee.

"What is it?" Dr. Satish asked.

"I don't know," she said. "It's just the whole situation."

"What do you mean? Are you concerned that she was so level

headed and not scared like other girls her age would have been?"

"No," Janet said waving off the notion. "She's always been more mature than, well, than people my even age sometimes." Dr. Satish looked at her somewhat confused. "It's just who it was that died."

"Was it someone close?"

"No," Janet said taking a deep breath. "The man who-" she paused trying to fit her thoughts into coherent words. "The man who killed her father and left her sister in the condition she's in. It was his sister-in-law."

Dr. Satish leaned back and looked at Janet, his mouth agape in surprise as the connections made sense. "That means the classmate she was visiting is-"

"His daughter, yes," she finished for him. "I didn't realize it until I knew who had died and found out Kimberly had been there."

"Are they close?" He asked. "I mean are they friends other than classmates?"

"It seems so," Janet said. "They seemed close the other night when we saw her and her mother at the hospital."

"The other night?" he asked. "I thought the aunt just died yesterday."

"She did, but they were at the hospital because the girl's mother had some kind of accident."

Dr. Satish nodded and took a sip of his own coffee. "Do they know?"

"Kimberly does," Janet said, her hand suddenly shaking. "She told me she'd known since school started, but it doesn't seem to bother her. She said it wouldn't matter, because she could avoid coming into contact with him and by the end of the year, she wouldn't have to share classes with the girl anymore."

"Well," Dr. Satish said. "There are two ways to look at this." Janet looked up at him hoping he had an easy solution to help her cope with the situation. "Either, you can be proud that your daughter is already planning to skip another grade, or you can be proud that she can control herself enough to look at a potential problem logically and see a resolution before the problem becomes a fact."

"Or I can sit here and worry that my daughter is consorting with the family of the man that destroyed ours."

"Mrs. Tucker," Dr. Satish said, placing a calming hand on hers. "You must remember that it was the man who caused so much devastation. His children are innocent in this and probably have been victimized by the event as well."

"But I cannot have my daughter going to his house," she said as the tears she was holding back finally broke free. "And despite the fact that his children may be innocent, I will not have the child of a murderer in this house."

"I do understand your feelings," he said, reaching over to place a reassuring hand on hers. "Unfortunately there is no easy solution."

"There is," Janet said, choking out a short laugh. "But I need a time machine and a way to get him to trade places with John and Kryssi."

"Sadly," Dr. Satish smiled. "My name is Satish, not Brown, and sadly I do not have a DeLorean outside." The joke had the desired effect and Janet again laughed in spite of herself. "Mrs. Tucker," he said as she wiped the tears from her face. "Talk with your daughter, be honest with her and let her know how you feel. She is exceptionally intelligent. Together the two of you can figure out a way to allow her to, if not be friends with the girl, then at least be proper classmates without risking an encounter with the child's father."

"There is always home schooling." Janet said as she rose to clear the now empty coffee cups.

"Do you think that is an option?" Dr. Satish said as he grabbed his bag.

"Of course," Janet said. "There is so much she could teach me." Dr. Satish laughed. The two of them continued talking for a short while, until he noticed the time and suggested that Janet show him to her daughter.

~*~

The examination took all of ten minutes. She stayed in the room watching the doctor as he checked Krystal's vital signs and reflexes. He checked her muscle tone and tried to get her to respond to different stimuli, such as sound, smells, and touch. She watched closely and took a mental note to try the same things tomorrow. After the doctor left, she picked up the laptop and again checked to make sure she wasn't being watched.

She opened a file she downloaded about a woman who killed her husband in a car accident. She read how the woman had tampered with the brakes on the car and even rode in the vehicle with him. Her injuries were serious from the accident, and when police learned of the brake tampering, she was excluded as a suspect. The investigation stalled and went cold until ten years later. The woman had gone to see her dentist and while under anesthesia told the doctor she had lost two of her teeth in the accident. The dentist had no knowledge of the accident so asked her about it and she confessed to tampering with the brakes and murdering her husband. She read on and discovered that the confession was inadmissible and the woman escaped prosecution on a legal technicality.

The article was good, but not exactly what she needed. She needed a plan that would prevent anyone from even suspecting her. It did give her an idea however. She searched the internet until she found a page that gave detailed descriptions of the brakes on vehicles and how they worked. She read how the cycle of pressing a foot on a pedal leads to compression of fluids and puts pads in motion to contact a spinning rotor, which slows and eventually stops the spinning. As she read this, an idea occurred to her.

'What if the brakes could be tampered with and leave no evidence that they were?' she thought. She searched her mind to see if she had ever read anything about the model of truck Jason McDowell drove. When the answer finally came to her, she spent the next two hours becoming intimately familiar with brake designs on a 1998 Ford F-150 pickup truck. She read articles and watched a video on how to flush the brake lines to replace the fluid. She made a note of the tools she would need and decided to test her newfound knowledge to see how easily she could perform such a feat.

Quickly making her plans, she wiped the browser's history and cleared all of its cookies before shutting down the laptop. She was happy that she had something to occupy her mind. With a small smile, she once again stepped into Krystal's room and noted the unsurprising lack of change in the child before turning to head upstairs to her room.

She changed into her pajamas and climbed into bed thinking about what she would do if her experiment were successful. Could she actually do it to someone, even someone as vile as Jason McDowell was? Could she bring herself to do something she knew would cause their death? That thought both frightened her and thrilled her at the same time. She lay in bed for an hour thinking over the possibilities.

In her mind, she saw the truck careening out of control and flying over the edge of a cliff. She then imagined the truck swerving all over the road and slamming into a building, McDowell screaming apologies as it burst into flames. She fell asleep that night thrilled with the idea of extinguishing the life of a person she had hated for three years. Fear, however, tempered that thrill. Her last conscious thought of the night was the fear that what she wanted to do could cause her guilt or give her nightmares for the rest of her life.

~*~

Billy came into the house and had to duck to avoid one of Joyce's favorite vases from hitting him in the head. Jason followed up with a beer bottle that broke right next to his brother's head. Billy stormed into the house and demanded to know why his brother was tearing up his house. Jason spun to face his brother.

"What?" Jason asked as he paused to catch his breath. "You think I'm just gonna sit here and vacuum your floors and do yer dishes while you screw my wife?"

"You're out of yer damned mind!" Billy shouted at his brother.

"I'm out of my mind? Who's the one who ten seconds after his wife dies is makin' moves on his brother's wife?"

"What the hell makes you think I want Angie?"

"I seen it all damned day!" Jason shouted. "Y'all was all lovey dovey this mornin', and then you had to have her help you at the funeral home."

"I did need her help," Billy said. "I won't be able to get through this shit without someone helpin' me make arrangements and figurin' out what needs to be done. You sure as hell ain't no help."

"So you figure you can jump into bed with yer sister-in-law and maybe she can make yer troubles go away?"

"Ain't nobody jumped in bed with nobody," Billy retorted. "'Cept maybe you and whatever skank you been hookin' up with lately."

Jason smiled as he looked his brother in the eye. "You didn't think she was a skank when you married her," he said.

If he had hit his brother with an electric shock, he couldn't have spurred him into action faster. Billy lunged at his brother hitting him in the gut with his shoulder and sending them both to the floor. Jason was still struggling to catch his breath when the first blow from Billy's fist landed on his forehead. That punch was followed by a quick succession of hits to his nose, mouth, eye, and jaw.

Jason became more dazed with each punch, but still had enough sense for his survival instincts to kick in, followed quickly by a kick to his brother's back. Billy didn't seem fazed by the blow and began choking Jason with one hand while the other continued to rain down blows. Jason's hand flung out and he blindly searched the floor nearby for something he could use to grant him even a moment of relief. His fingers found the neck of a beer bottle sticking out from under the edge of the sofa and he grabbed for it.

When the hard glass connected with Billy's temple, stars exploded behind his eyes and he felt the sharp glass fall to his shoulder before continuing to the floor. Jason took the opportunity to buck his brother off him and start his own assault. He had landed his fifth punch when he heard Angela scream for him to stop. He looked up to see her kneeling in front of him with her hands out, pleading for him to stop hitting Billy.

Her need to protect another man infuriated him even more and he started to lunge for her. He barely got his hand wrapped around her wrist when he felt the entire planet land on the back of his head. The last thing he heard before blackness conquered him was Angela screaming, "Mindy don't!"

~*~

FIVE

Kimberly paused when she entered the classroom. Mindy and Kelly were both already here. Lesley sat between the girls and was holding Kelly's hand as she and Mindy talked. Mindy had been out of school since her aunt's death to grieve with her family. Kelly had been out because finding the woman had been traumatic for her. Kimberly made her way over to the three girls and placed a hand on Mindy's shoulder.

"How are you doing?" she asked the girl, concern showing in her voice.

"Okay," Mindy said as she got up to hug the other girl. "Uncle Billy's been having the hardest time."

"He's her husband?" Kimberly asked. Mindy nodded as the two of them sat down. Kimberly turned to Kelly and took hold of her free hand. "How about you?" Kelly shrugged and looked down at her hands.

"She hasn't said anything since that day," Lesley said. "They have her on some medicine for her nerves, but…"

"Kelly, I'm so sorry," Kimberly said. "I should have called or something." Kelly shook her head and looked down frowning. "Hey," Kimberly whispered. "I know it still seems scary, but I promise someday it won't be as bad." Kelly nodded. "We're all here for you and we all need to be here for Mindy, too, yeah?" Kelly nodded again and leaned over into a group hug with her three friends.

Once the class officially started, Kimberly divided her attention between Mrs. Estep and Mindy McDowell. Throughout the class, Kimberly wondered if the other girl knew how happy she was that her aunt's death might be causing her father pain. She also wondered if it was possible that the girl didn't really know what kind of a monster her father truly was.

It wasn't until lunch that Kimberly remembered that the McDowell family members weren't the only ones affected by Mrs. McDowell's death. She began paying closer attention to Kelly and wondering what it was about that day that suddenly caused her friend to stop talking. She made a mental note to remember to ask her mother about it this evening.

By recess, Kimberly had watched enough of her friends to realize she would need to keep an eye on both of them. She doubted Mindy would need much looking after, but she would still keep an eye on her. Kelly, however, was in serious need of a friend; a real friend. Kimberly decided that she would do everything she could to be that friend for the poor girl.

By the time school let out, Kimberly had added several items to her list of things to research. She said goodbye to her friends, and after Mindy and Lesley departed, she took Kelly by the hand and looked the girl in the eye.

"Kelly," she said. "I am really sorry that I have been a lousy friend up until now. But I promise you that no matter what, I'm gonna be here for you from now on, okay?" Kelly nodded as a tear slid down her cheek, and the girls hugged. "Is it okay if I call you later?" Kimberly asked. "You don't have to talk or anything unless you want to. I just want to make sure you're okay."

Kelly nodded again and dug through her backpack for a pencil while Kimberly fished out a piece of paper. Kelly had just finished scrawling her number down when Kimberly's mother pulled into the parking lot with a black sedan right behind her. As Kimberly went to her mother's car, Kelly went to the black car and waved before getting in.

~*~

Janet sighed as she pulled to the curb in front of her house. She never could figure out why her father always parked beside his wife when they visited in separate cars. If she had pulled into the drive she would just have to come back out to let one of them out, but then parking at the curb meant she would have to come back out as well. Within the town of Piedmont Acres, it was illegal to park on the street after dark. As she and Kimberly made their way into the house, she wondered why her father was visiting in the first place.

"There they are," Adam Greene said as they walked in.

"Hi, Grandpa," Kimberly said, going to him for a hug.

"Hey, sweetheart," he said as he wrapped his arms around her. "How was school?"

"Good," she said, and then with a smile added, "I managed to stay awake."

"Well that's a positive sign, yeah?"

Kimberly giggled as she gave her grandmother a hug and then went into the den to spend some time with Krystal, while she pretended to do her homework. The truth was Kimberly had her homework finished before the final bell rang today, so she could spend all night with Krystal if she wanted.

Once the eight-year-old was out of sight Adam turned to his daughter and cleared his throat.

"And there's the look of impending bad news," Janet said as she shook her head. "What's wrong, Daddy?"

"Maybe you should get a cup of tea before we talk," Adam said.

"Oh God, Daddy, just tell me," Janet said as she leaned back onto the sofa.

"Go ahead, Adam," Jean said as she rose to her feet. "I'll get us some tea." As Jean walked into the kitchen, Adam looked at his daughter and gave a little sigh.

"Sweetie, I got a call today from EquiSure."

"Christ," Janet scoffed. "What now? Do they want to stop paying for her food and medicine?"

"No," Adam said quickly. "It wasn't about Kryssi."

"What was it then?" she asked as her mother set a cup of tea in front of her.

"It's about John's policy."

"What about it?"

"It seems they had an accounting error when they started cutting your checks," Adam began. "As you remember, they agreed to pay you from the day John died until the first check arrived six months later."

"Yes," Janet said warily.

"Well, sweetheart, it seems that they never adjusted back to the proper monthly payment for the annuity."

"What does that mean?" Janet asked shaking her head.

"It means that they have been over paying you since the second check for over three years," Adam said holding his breath for the eventual explosion. When none came, he exhaled slowly. "It also means," He carefully added, "That at the current rate, there is only enough money left on John's policy to pay out next month."

Janet gasped and sat up straight. "Next month," she exclaimed. "That's insane! They can't just stop all payments with a month's notice like that!"

"Now hold on, honey," Adam said holding his hands up defensively. "If you are willing to take the proper disbursement until the policy expires, you will have payments coming in for three more years."

"How much are the regular disbursements?" Janet asked.

"About nine hundred twenty-five dollars," Adam said.

"Daddy," she said. "The mortgage alone is eleven-hundred a month. Then there's Kimberly's school supplies, clothes, stuff we need around the house, Kryssi's meds that your savings account doesn't cover..."

"I know, sweetie," Adam said. "And EquiSure has considered that your expenses may exceed the reduced payment."

"I'm sure that doesn't mean they're going to keep paying me

sixty-five hundred a month."

"Well," Adam said. "They have offered you three possible solutions. Either you can take a lump sum payment of the remainder of the funds, which will equal about eighty-five hundred dollars."

"Or," Janet prompted after a pause.

"Or," Adam continued. "They can continue your current payments through November, at which time you will receive your final payment from them, which would still be quite a bit smaller than you are accustomed. That is if you do not want to take the third option, which would be the reduced payments."

"So this is it?" Janet asked. "They make a mistake and allow us to live comfortably for three years then pull the rug from under us?"

"Sweetie," Adam said. "It was an accounting error on their part. But legally yes, they have every right to do it."

Janet was in shock. She had just started feeling some sense of normalcy having both of her daughters home again. Now that normalcy was about to be uprooted.

"Daddy," she said nearly gasping for air. "What am I going to do?"

"Well, you'll need to get a job, certainly," Adam said, calmly. "Your mother and I can help with Kryssi, but financially, we put everything we could spare into her savings account."

"I haven't worked in three years," Janet gasped. "I wouldn't even know where to start."

"Why not try Greenholdt?" Jean asked as she took a sip of her own tea. "Surely they would give you your old job back."

"Greenholdt," Janet said. "Mom I didn't even give them notice. I just never went back in after John died."

"I talked to Mrs. Adams earlier," Adam said. "She remembers that you did great work for them before, and she understands why you left the way you did. She would love to have you back."

"You applied for a job on my behalf?" Janet asked almost insulted.

"No, sweetie," he said. "I asked your old friend if she would be interested in giving you the opportunity to apply."

Janet sat and thought for a while. No matter how she looked at it, she needed to go back to work. It also appeared that she could get her old job back simply by asking for it. It bothered her that this situation came up on her so unexpectedly. It bothered her more that she was so emotionally unprepared for this kind of surprise. She thought about her parents' offer to help with Krystal while she worked, and then thought of something else.

"Mom, Dad, if go back to Greenholdt Construction, I will be working until past time to pick up Kimberly from school."

"I can always ride the bus," Kimberly said, surprising them all when she entered the room. "Plus, unless I was seeing things when we got home, Grandma and Grandpa both have cars."

Janet gave an exasperated sigh and looked from her daughter to her parents. "I'll make arrangements tomorrow for you to start taking the bus, and talk to Chrys about coming back to work."

Adam and Jean smiled as Adam handed the phone to his daughter. "She's waiting for your call now."

"You are a manipulator," she said as she snatched the device from his hand.

"I didn't manipulate you," he said defensively.

"I meant you manipulated Chrys into taking me back and waiting for me to call her."

"Well," Adam said as he leaned back and motioned for Kimberly to come sit in his lap. "I do what I can for my girls."

Janet shook her head as the other end of the line connected. "Hello, Can I speak with Chrystal Adams?"

~*~

Billy sat on the end of the loading dock and opened his lunch pail. When he pulled out the first sandwich, he didn't bother to look it over. Try as she might, Angela never got his sandwiches just right. Joyce knew just the right combination of mayonnaise and mustard to put on his bologna. He almost gagged on the amount of mayo in that first bite, but kept with it, hoping she would get the formula right one day.

Halfway through his second sandwich, he looked up to find his brother staring at him from the other side of the tarmac. Seeing that he had been noticed, Jason came over to the loading dock and propped a foot on a pallet leaning against the wall.

"Still pissed?" he asked as Billy took another bite of his sandwich.

"Wouldn't you be?"

131

"Look," Jason said. "I know you wouldn't screw around with Angie. I was just pissed off and then the more I got drunk the more things made sense."

"That alone should tell you it's time for you to quit drinkin'" Billy said washing the taste of the sandwich down.

"Maybe," Jason said. "Look, I wanna come by and see the kids."

"Come by sober, and no problem."

"Won't be a problem," Jason said and Billy looked at him with a brow raised. "I started workin' at Greenholdt today. They do random drug tests. If I come to work hung over, I lose the job."

"Hm," Billy said opening his third sandwich. "Well, come by tonight... sober, and we'll have some supper."

"A'ight," Jason said as he turned to leave.

"Jase," Billy called after him. When his brother turned back, he shook his head slightly. "Be ready to make it up to yer wife, too." Jason nodded as he turned again to leave. Billy watched as the tan pickup left the parking lot and turned onto the main road.

She slipped into the garage from the kitchen door and closed it quietly. She would only have a few minutes to do this, but she wanted to make sure it was done right. The last thing she needed was the blue Taurus to malfunction on the way to school or work. She unlocked the door and reached in to pull the hood latch. After putting the key into the ignition and turning it almost all the way, she slipped back out of the car and crawled underneath. She found the first connector almost immediately, precisely where the diagrams said it would be.

She held the empty soda bottle underneath the line and loosened the connector. It was harder than she thought it would be which made sense, as no one would want this particular area to be loose. Once the connection was severed, she put the end of the small hose into the bottle and allowed the red fluid to drain into it. She waited a few seconds after the last drop fell, and reconnected the line to the brake, making sure to tighten it completely. She then slid down to the back tire and repeated the process.

Once she had drained all four lines, she lifted the hood and searched for the white oval like cap that would be the brake fluid reservoir. She found one the right shape, but this one was black and it took her a few moments squinting into the darkened area to make out the words. This was precisely what she was looking for and she opened the cap and then dumped the content of the bottle in. After replacing the cap, she quietly lowered the hood and pressed hard until she heard and felt the latch catch.

Finally, she slid back into the car and pressed the brake pedal. It went all the way to the floor with no resistance. She pressed again with the same results. Five times, she pressed the brake pedal until finally she felt some resistance returning to them. By the tenth press of the pedal, she felt the full resistance of the brakes catching, indicating the lines to be full. She pressed them a few more times to be certain before finally turning the key switch all the way off and removing the key. She pressed the lock plunger down, not wanting to risk being heard if she used the auto lock button on the key ring.

As she re-entered the house, she felt her heart racing. This can be done, she thought. The fear and excitement of that knowledge brought a smile to her face. She went into the den, picked up the laptop, and began erasing every trace of her research before heading back into the living room.

~*~

Krystal was just putting the mayonnaise in the refrigerator when Janet walked into the kitchen. Grabbing her sandwich, she headed for the door to return to the den, but her mother stopped her.

"Where were you?" Janet asked.

"Upstairs," Kimberly answered. "Why?"

"I didn't even think to look there," her mother said. "I came back upstairs and you weren't in the den."

"Sorry," Kimberly said. "I didn't think to let you know."

"No, don't worry, sweetie," Janet said. "I just wondered where you got off to."

Kimberly sat at the counter with her sandwich and began reading her book. Janet tossed a bottle into the trash and went into the den to check on Krystal. She checked the child's vital signs first and then performed her daily exercises. This part always took the longest time, as Janet made sure to check the child's muscle tone before and after flexing and stretching her legs and arms.

After completing the range of motion exercises, Janet got a can of the nutritional supplement from the mini-fridge in the room.

While it warmed, she checked Krystal's catheter and other tubes. Once she got the child's dinner started, she chanced sitting on the bed beside her and began rubbing her daughter's arm.

"Oh, Kryssi," she said. "I am so sorry that things are so messed up." She brought her hand up to smooth out the child's hair. "But with Grandma and Grandpa looking after you, I can do a little work and maybe keep us out of trouble."

Janet watched the child as she continued caressing her arm. She wished so much that Krystal would wake. She knew that if this miracle could happen, then everything else would be all right. "What I wouldn't give to have you back with us," she whispered. "And have that bastard that did this to you in the ground." Krystal's lip twitched slightly and Janet jumped. "Kryssi?" she whispered. "Can you hear me?"

Krystal lay on the bed immobile, no indication that she had ever reacted. Janet searched the child's face and gently shook her but got no response. "Kryssi," she whispered again. "Please come back to Mommy," she continued, grabbing the child's hand and watching her face, hoping for another sign. "Please come home," she pleaded. "I promise I would do anything to have you back. I'd give up this house and live on the streets. I'd give up everything. I'd kill that bastard myself and give up my freedom if you'd just come back."

There it was. Another twitch of the child's mouth gave her mother just a little more hope. Janet began crying as she continued. "I would bury him in that damned truck of his and set it on fire to give you the justice you need to come back home." This time Krystal's whole face twitched and Janet felt a finger move under her hand.

"Oh God," Janet sobbed. Realization dawned, as she understood at last what her daughter needed to come out of this coma. She looked around the room before returning her attention to her daughter. Finally, she leaned down and whispered in the girl's ear. "Do you want Mommy to kill Jason McDowell?" Janet's heart leapt as the tiny hand closed on her fingers. She laid her head on the pillow beside her daughter's head and wept. She was still there when darkness crept into the room. She was there the next morning when Kimberly came downstairs to breakfast.

The moon was in its first quarter and didn't give very much light to her path. In spite of the occasional tripping, she didn't mind the darkened areas. She knew precisely where she was going and mapped out the directions in her head. She felt it would be safer getting there on foot so there would be less chance of someone knowing she was there.

It had been five days since she tested her knowledge of brakes on the Taurus, and she spent that entire time familiarizing herself with the braking system of a 1998 Ford F150. This was the truck model that Jason McDowell drove. The same truck destroyed her family. The same truck would destroy the man himself.

At the end of the block, she saw that her target was practically cloaked in darkness. Most of the streetlights were out on this side of the street, so she made her way quickly to the house she sought. Once there, she crouched behind the tree a few feet from the front steps. Although the lights were on in the living room and upstairs, no one seemed to be near the windows. She peered around the other side of the tree and saw the pickup truck parked right behind the old car with the busted window. Quickly she darted to the truck and slid underneath. Unlike with the Taurus, this time she started with the back brake lines, emptying the fluid into her bottle.

She worked quickly but made sure that the connectors were tight before scooting to the front of the truck and going to work on the front brakes. Just as she tightened the last brake line, she heard someone say "Slow down," just before the front door closed. Her heart slammed into her throat as the screen door slammed on the frame. She saw two sets of feet walking towards the truck and stop before hearing the driver's side door open.

"Hop in, JJ," she heard a voice say. "Let's go get them pizzas."

Her heart began hammering as the second pair of feet disappeared into the truck. She scooted quickly out from under the truck and then under the car in front of it. She kept scooting until she couldn't scoot anymore. Fearing she could still be seen, she bent her knees and lay under the vehicle hoping she was completely out of sight.

She let out a gasp as she heard the truck roar to life. Sweat began pouring down her face as she listened to the vehicle slip into gear and back out of the driveway. She continued to lie there for at least two minutes after the sounds of the truck vanished, hoping they wouldn't return before she got out of there.

She finally began wiggling out from under the car and cleared the back bumper. She looked around quickly, saw no one on the street or sidewalks, and got to her feet while remaining crouched. She quickly slipped out of the yard and straightened up as she began passing the other houses on the street. She needed to hurry now. She'd been gone too long. She ran for the next street and then began threading her way through the back yards between Willowood Dr. and her home.

Running and stumbling for the next twenty minutes, she was near panic when she realized the yard she just ran through was her own. She quickly doubled back and peered through the window of her back door. Seeing no one, she quietly slipped back inside and tiptoed into the den. Peering into the room, she let out a soft sigh as she noted everything was exactly as she left it.

She made her way upstairs and shed her clothes. They were ruined now. She had a hole in her jeans and there were oil streaks on her shirt. She looked in the mirror and saw dirt and oil streaked on her face, neck, and arms. She grabbed up her old clothes and took them downstairs to the basement. The work area of the basement was packed with stuff they had stored or no longer used, so she figured it would be safe to leave them hidden down here until she could find a way to burn them.

Once she was back upstairs, she jumped into the shower and scrubbed herself clean. She was halfway through drying her hair when a thought occurred to her. 'JJ,' she thought. 'The little boy is in that truck.' Her heart began hammering again as she realized her error. No one was supposed to be in that truck but Jason. 'Oh God, what-' suddenly another thought occurred to her. 'He basically took two people from me,' she mused. 'Why not take another person from him? Show him what it's like to lose a child just as he loses his life.'

With that thought, she continued drying her hair and brushed it. A smile lightened her face as she imagined the look of horror on Jason McDowell's face when he realized the he was about to lose his son and his own life. Once she was properly cleaned, she slipped into her pajamas and rushed back downstairs. In the den, she lay on the bed where she had been before sneaking out to murder the worst enemy her family had ever known. As sleep wrapped around her, the thrill of her activity coursed through her once more.

Jason stepped out of the shower and grabbed the towel. Halfway through drying himself off, he heard a soft knock on the door. "Still naked," he called out. The door opened slightly and Angela leaned in. "Hey, babe," he said with a lopsided grin.

"Jase, the kids want to know if they can have pizza for supper tonight," she said, worried he might demand some beer as well.

"Yeah," he said. "Call it in and have Billy go pick it up. My wallet's on the bed."

A few minutes later, a freshly dressed Jason McDowell came downstairs. Angela was just hanging up the phone and handed

Jason his wallet.

"They said it is gonna be thirty-five even," she said. "I didn't get it out yet." Jason pulled two twenties out of his wallet and handed them to Billy. "I got you a Meat Lovers," Angela told him as he put his wallet back in his pocket.

"Good," Jason said.

"Daddy, can I go with Uncle Billy?" JJ asked.

"If he don't care," Jason said with a smile. This is the way things should be, with his family giving him the respect he deserved.

"I gotta stop and get some gas," Billy said.

"The Ford's full," said Jason. "Take it." He tossed Billy the keys.

Billy merely shrugged and looked at his nephew. "Got yer shoes on?"

"Yep," JJ said as he ran to the front door.

"Slow down," Billy said, as he and Jason Junior stepped outside. The two went straight for the tan pickup and Billy opened the driver's side door. "Hop in, JJ," Billy said. "Let's go get them pizzas."

Once they were in the truck, Billy reached over to pull JJ's seatbelt onto him. He tried several times but could not get the buckle to latch. He sighed as the belt kept trying to slip back into place.

"We'll just have to risk it," he said. "Just hold it like this so it looks like it's on, and sit still."

"Okay," JJ said as Billy started the truck. Billy eased out onto the street, put the truck into drive, and they were off to Pizza Hut.

In no time, Billy was going fifty miles an hour down Main Street. He was coming up on the intersection of Main and Fourth Avenue when he saw the light change. He tried the brakes only to find no response from them.

"Shit," he said, pumping the brakes again. He zoomed through the intersection against the light and kept pumping the brakes. He continued to get no response as he again blew through a red light at Third Avenue. Near panic, he shut off the ignition and breathed a sigh of relief as the truck slowed down and finally came to a stop right on the railroad tracks between Third Avenue and Second. "That was scary," he said to JJ as he turned the ignition. The motor didn't turn over. He tried again and a cold sweat broke out as the lights on the railroad crossing began to flash and the gates started down.

"Shit," Billy said again, trying the ignition a third time. He heard the horn of the train and knew he had to do something. He thought quickly and nearly soiled his pants when the train horn blew even louder and closer. He looked at the gearshift and groaned as he slammed it into park and tried the ignition again. The truck roared to life and he jerked the transmission into gear and broke through the barricade just as the train whipped past them.

Billy's heart was pounding as he came upon Second Avenue and he looked over at JJ and smiled. As he pressed the brakes, he suddenly remembered why he had been stuck on the tracks to begin with. He saw the light change and knew he didn't have enough time to shut off the engine and coast to a stop, so he pumped the brakes frantically, hoping to either stop or get through the intersection before any traffic came from the other direction.

Just before he passed under the light, Billy felt the brakes catch and he began to stop. His relief was short lived however as an eighteen-wheeler slammed into the passenger side of the pickup. Billy felt JJ slam into him and saw the boy enter his vision just before the impact sent the truck into oncoming traffic. The last thing Billy saw was a headlight just before the car it belonged to slammed into his door.

Jason sat at the table, the soda in his hand bubbling as his hand shook. It had been three days since he had a drink and he was starting to feel the effects of being sober. Angela looked over at him as he stared down into his drink. She thought he might be going through delirium tremens, or DTs. Just as she was about to give him a valium to calm himself down, there was a knock on the door. Janet opened the door to find two police officers on the porch.

"Mrs. McDowell?" the young officer said.

"Yes," she replied.

"I'm afraid I have some bad news about your husband."

"Jason," she called as she turned her back on the officers.

"Yeah," he answered.

"There is someone who wants to talk to you." She turned back to the officers and sighed. "I'm not sure what he did," she said to them. "But he's been trying to clean up. He hasn't drank anything in a couple of days and-"

"What's goin' on?" Jason said from behind her.

The officers looked at each other for a second before the young dark haired one turned back to them. "Mr. McDowell," he said. "I'm Officer Morrow. Do you own a 1998 tan Ford F150 pickup?"

"Yeah," Jason said. "My brother's out with it pickin' up some food. Why?"

"Sir," Officer Morrow said. "I'm afraid there's been an accident."

Angela let out a scream. "JJ?" she said, shoving Jason out of the way. "Is my son alright?"

"Ma'am," Officer Morrow said. "You should sit down."

"No!" Angela screamed as she collapsed to the floor. Jason looked from his wife to the police officers in confusion.

"I don't understand," Jason said in shock. "What's goin on? What'd Billy do to my truck?"

~*~

SIX

Mindy was at a loss. Her brother was dead. 'Killed on impact,' they said. Her mother was sobbing uncontrollably, too grief stricken to put words to her prayers. Her father just stood there numbly, still not fully comprehending what had happened. Mindy, herself, wept fiercely for not just her brother, but also her uncle who cared more for her than her own father.

Mindy barely heard the officers when they offered to drive them to the hospital to be with Uncle Billy and to see to JJ's body. She heard her mother sob even louder and saw her dad nod. Mindy looked around the living room for something, she couldn't think of what. She walked behind the officer as he helped her mother to the sofa and sat beside her. She wanted her mom to put her arms around her and tell her she was having a nightmare, but the woman's continued sobbing told her it would be a lie.

Someone was saying something and she thought she heard someone mention her uncle's name. She looked to the front door hoping to see him and JJ walk through it and that this was all a huge mistake. Neither Billy nor JJ came in. Instead, two other people walked in. They were wearing lighter uniforms than the police officers were. Somewhere in the back of her mind, Mindy heard the word 'ambulance', but she couldn't for the life of her figure out what the word could mean.

She heard a woman's voice, which sounded as though it was

coming from down the street, saying, "Look at me, please." However, she had no idea who was speaking. Suddenly, someone had their hand on her chin and turned her head. Her vision was half obscured by a blinding light that flashed in front of one eye and then the next. 'Am I dying, too?' she thought. 'Or am I just going blind?' The woman's voice from down the street spoke again, asking, "Can you tell me your name?"

As her vision cleared, she saw a woman in front of her in the light blue uniform that she found familiar. She saw the woman's lips move and a moment later heard the voice from down the street ask, "Do you understand me?" The woman in front of her looked to her left and her lips moved again. Again, a few minutes later, Mindy heard the distant voice say, "We should take them both in. I think they're in shock."

What happened next was a blur of movement and emotions. Some of it felt surreal and some parts felt all too real. Somewhere in the back of her mind, Mindy realized she'd been picked up and carried outside. She watched her mother being laid on a bed with wheels, crying louder than she'd ever cried before. She saw her dad look at her with a puzzled expression as she passed by him, the words "I don't understand," escaping his lips.

Mindy would not remember being put into the ambulance or being buckled into a seat. She would not remember the ride to the hospital or anything that happened there. For the rest of her life, the only thing from this night that Mindy would remember would be her mother lying on the wheeled bed, writhing and crying as if she were dying.

~*~

Monday morning found Kimberly in the bed with her sister and Janet lying on the sofa on the other side of the room. The two of them had spent the past two nights sleeping in Krystal's bedroom hoping for another indication she would be waking. Janet called Dr. Satish Saturday evening and he promised to stop by on his way home, this evening. In the meantime, the two of them had to get dressed. Kimberly had school and Janet needed to start her first day at work.

After dropping Kimberly off at school, Janet headed east toward the commercial area of Piedmont Acres. She passed the restaurants that were on the outskirts of the district, which only served to remind her that she had skipped breakfast this morning. The closer she got to the Greenholdt building, the more nervous she became. She hadn't worked in three years and it was only just occurring to her that many things may have changed in that time.

Her nerves nearly had her convinced to turn around and go home when she pulled up to the entrance of Greenholdt's parking lot. As she pulled into a space, she looked at the three-story building that passed for a high rise in this town. She sat in her car for five minutes before resigning herself with a sigh to go inside and get it over with before she completely lost her nerve.

Chrystal Adams was waiting for her when Janet walked into the building's lobby. Her warm smile had an instant calming effect on Janet, which propelled her further into the building. The two met halfway and shared a hug before Chrystal held her at arms-length. The woman's long hair was still the same red tint it was when they had graduated college together, and her eyes were just as blue and clear.

Janet felt a slight touch of jealousy as she touched her own greying hair. She realized this morning that the past three years had taken their toll on her appearance. John had fallen in love with her once honey blonde hair, but that would only return with the help of a talented colorist. She recalled noticing that her brown eyes seemed darker to her, and less welcoming. The most glaring change she felt when facing her old friend were the wrinkles she tried to conceal before leaving the house. Those tiny creases across her forehead and around her eyes and mouth seemed to her to have magically appeared, but were, as she knew, the result of three years of worrying, crying and stressing over the shambles she felt her life had become.

"I am so glad you're back," Chrystal said, interrupting Janet's mental criticism of herself. "I haven't had anyone decent to talk to since you left."

"Well you may change your mind about that, if I mess up your new computer system," Janet said.

"Oh you won't. It's the same system as before, just new computers."

The two women laughed as Chrystal led the way to her office so Janet could fill out the necessary paperwork.

~*~

"Shane, you got that report from Friday night's MVA?" Officer Keith Rogan asked. Officer Morrow looked up from the file and nodded. He was glad for the interruption as his eyes were starting to burn from filling out the incident reports and getting his logs straight. "Here's the truck driver's statement," Rogan said as he handed more papers over."

"How's he doing, by the way?" Morrow asked.

Rogan grunted and said, "He called his boss and quit, then called his wife to meet him at the bus stop. He says he's never driving anything again. He's probably home now trying to find a work from home job."

"Well, I can understand how he feels," Morrow said looking over the statement. "Looks like it wasn't his fault, but he still hit a vehicle that caused a kid to die."

"About that kid," Rogan said. "Weren't we just at that house last week?"

Morrow nodded as he rubbed his eyes. "Yeah," he said. "It was the driver's wife that fell from the roof."

"Glad I'm not in that family," Rogan said. "Looks like the guy's touch and go at the hospital."

"Yeah, there's something weird about this though."

"Weird?"

"Yeah," Morrow said as he spun the truck driver's statement around for Rogan to read it. "The truck driver says he saw the guy hit the brakes too late when they were headed to the intersection, but he didn't have time to hit his brakes."

"You think he's lying?"

"No," Morrow said as he brought out another sheet. "Look here. The woman travelling behind McDowell said she saw him break through the barricade on the tracks just before he passed her at the gas station. She said it looked like he had stalled there after coasting to a stop."

"So, what, you think he was having engine trouble?"

"Maybe, I don't know."

"I think you're just looking for something because of the freakiness of the past couple of weeks," Rogan said as he got to his feet.

"Maybe," Morrow said. "I'm gonna look over the wife's report too, to see if there's anything."

"You're wasting your time, Cochise," Rogan said, tossing a ball of paper into the trash as he left the squad room.

Morrow looked over the statements again and tried to find what it was that was needling the back of his mind. After a few minutes of re-reading the same words, he put all of the paperwork in place and placed the file in his pigeonhole. He went downstairs where PAPD had set up their recently assembled CSI unit. When he walked in he saw the unit commander and walked up to him, unsure of how to ask him for what he needed.

"Officer Morrow," the commander said when he noticed the young patrol officer enter. "What brings you to the dungeons?"

Morrow smiled and rubbed his finger across his lower lip before responding. "Look," he began and then changed his mind. "I'm sorry. I can't remember your name."

"Ben," the commander said.

"Ben," Morrow repeated. "I know that it's usually the detectives who ask you to take a look at things, but I know you guys are already going over the MVA from last night, right?"

"Yes we are," Ben said. "Have you come across something that makes you think we should be looking at something specific?"

"Kind of," Morrow said with a wince.

"Kind of?"

"Well, yeah. I mean I don't know if my suspicions will taint your perception of the evidence or…"

"I wish people would stop taking those shows so seriously," Ben said shaking his head. "Just tell me what you know."

"Nothing," Morrow said raising his hands slightly. "I mean I have a couple of witness statements that make me think that maybe the pickup was having some kind of trouble."

"Like what?"

"I'd initially say engine trouble," Morrow said. "But something about the way they said he was driving reminds me of when I was just starting to drive and my brakes went out. I had to turn off my engine to get the car stopped and… Well, I didn't have any accidents, but having done it, I can get how people could think he was having engine trouble."

"So we should check his brakes?"

"I mean, I can't recommend that can I?"

"You are a responding officer to the event," Ben said. "You

have access to first-hand information that even the detectives may not have at this time. Any of that information you feel will help us collect functional evidence is welcome."

"Okay then," Morrow said breathing a little easier. "I mean it may be nothing, but at least we'll know."

Ben smiled as the officer started to back out of the work area. "At least we'll know," he said.

As Officer Morrow made his way back up to the squad room, he thought again about Joyce McDowell's accident. He went to one of the patrol desks and logged into the system. In no time, he had the incident file on the screen and began reading. He was slightly surprised to see the autopsy report already in, and clicked on that file.

According to the Medical Examiner, Joyce McDowell suffered traumatic damage to her head, neck, and thoracic region. Several bones were broken along her neck and back as well as her skull. Morrow was surprised, however, that the M.E. listed her cause of death as exsanguination. Upon reading further, he saw that the hospital had removed several pieces of glass from her neck, one of which had pierced her carotid artery.

'Must have been from the windshield, when her head hit it,' he said to himself. Other than the rushed autopsy, Morrow couldn't find anything in the report that tied to her husband's accident last night. 'Maybe Keith's right and it's all just a freaky coincidence.' Morrow closed the files and signed off the system before clocking out and heading home for some much needed sleep.

~*~

Janet pulled into the school parking lot with a huge grin on her face. Nervous as she was when she got to work this morning, she found that she had barely missed a step in the day-to-day operations. She was exhilarated being back at work. She knew there would need to be some adjusting, but for now, she just wanted to concentrate on today.

She pulled up to the front of the building to find Kimberly and two other girls huddled together. Each girl had a somber look on her faces. None of them looked up when she stopped, so she tapped her horn to get her daughter's attention. The girls looked up and Janet saw tears flowing down the cheeks of the two girls with her daughter. Janet quickly became concerned, but her daughter rose and came to the car.

"What's wrong with them?" she asked her daughter as Kimberly got into the car.

"Mindy's brother and uncle were in a car wreck Saturday night," Kimberly said.

"Mindy…" Janet thought for a second. "You mean Mindy, the McDowell girl?"

"Yeah," Kimberly said as she buckled her seat belt. The little girl turned to wave at her friends and Janet put the car in motion.

Janet's earlier joy at being back to work was a thing of the past. "Is- are they alright?" she asked.

"JJ is dead," Kimberly said as she began leafing through her book. "Her uncle might die soon. They said he was badly hurt. Too bad they got the wrong Mr. McDowell though." Janet looked at her daughter in shock for a moment before remembering to pay attention to the road.

"You shouldn't say things like that," Janet scolded. "You should never want to see anyone hurt."

"Not even him?"

Janet felt the bile rising in her throat and had to swallow repeatedly before committing what she considered the ultimate hypocrisy. "Not even him," she said through gritted teeth.

Janet drove on toward the house, her mind swirling with possibilities. 'This is precisely the kind of justice the bastard deserves,' she thought. 'Let him lose everyone he loves before he gets what's coming to him.'

Beside her, Kimberly was thinking the exact same thing. She enjoyed the idea that Jason McDowell was suffering. As she pictured him lying in bed crying over the loss of his brother and son, another thought entered her mind. She had never hated before. In spite of being the quiet one and the one who preferred to be left alone, Kimberly had always loved, if not as openly, then surely as deeply as her sister had.

The realization that she not only hated someone, but also relished in her hatred of him was somewhat unsettling for the little girl. She looked over at her mother who was concentrating on driving and decided it wouldn't hurt to ask about her hate.

"How much can you hate someone before it makes you bad?" she asked.

"What do you mean, 'makes you bad'?" Janet asked, glancing at her daughter.

"I mean, I hate Mindy's dad so much that I want him to die like he made Daddy die."

"Honey," Janet said. "Hating someone doesn't make you bad. What you do with your hate decides whether you're good or bad."

"So if I wish he died would that be bad?"

Janet smiled at that question. It wasn't often, especially lately, that the girl needed her mother's help figuring something out. It made Janet happy that she could still teach her daughter something. "No, honey," She said. She remembered something John told her when he was making plans to go out on his own as an architect. "You're daddy always said that wishing doesn't make anything come true, only good planning and execution." Kimberly gave her mother a puzzled look before returning to her book. "At least that Mindy girl won't be around you for another week or so," Janet mumbled. The two rode the rest of the way home in silence.

She sat on the sofa and opened the laptop. This time she began searching psychology. She worried that the unintentional death she caused might cause her to have nightmares. In spite of the fact that she actually did cause the accident, she still had a hard time believing that she was responsible for the little boy's death. Her heart nearly stopped when she found out that not only did she miss Jason with the improvised brake job, but she killed his son as well. The shock of the news thankfully didn't show on her face, but it still hadn't worn off yet. She knew, that night, that it was altogether possible that the boy would die, but the news that it actually happened still shook her some.

'Why wasn't it on the news?' she asked herself. 'You'd think a kid dying in an accident would be the leading story.' With that thought in mind, she brought up the website for the town's newspaper, The Piedmont Herald. She scanned the lead stories and found no mention of the accident. Clocking the search box, she typed in McDowell and hit enter. The search brought up a list of articles from three years ago, all surrounding the death of John Tucker and the trial of Jason McDowell. She couldn't find anything concerning Friday's accident.

She went to her favorite search website and typed in McDowell dies in car accident. She was surprised that the closest thing she could find was a wreck in Connecticut from last year. She took it as an omen that no one cared about what happened to that family. As she dwelled on that thought for a moment, a new plan formed in her mind. 'Does he care about what happens?' she thought. She began searching again for information. 'Good planning and execution,' she thought. 'That's all I need.' If she did everything right, everyone in the McDowell family would be out of her life.

She began reading an article about poisonings and saw one item where a man poisoned his children with brake fluid. Her head snapped up. She quickly cleared the browser history and cache. Once she closed the browser, she closed the laptop and jumped up from the sofa. She quickly made her way downstairs to where she had hidden her dirty clothes from Friday. She searched the box and her clothes and found nothing. Thinking quickly, she ran upstairs to her bedroom.

There it was, plain as day on her dresser. The bottle of brake fluid that she didn't get to put back into the pickup. She snatched the bottle up and took it into the bathroom where she then emptied it into the toilet. Once she flushed the evidence down, she thought about what to do with the bottle itself. She took it back downstairs to the basement and tucked it behind her clothes, making a mental note to dispose of everything tonight. Once finished, she headed back upstairs to work on her plan.

Janet and Kimberly had just sat down to a dinner of cold cut sandwiches. It wasn't a traditional dinner, but her first day back at work, light as it was, had still drained Janet. In addition to that, finding out that Jason McDowell's son was dead and his brother nearly so, was playing on her nerves. She really wished she knew what the police knew about the accident. With their history, it was only a matter of time before they began to suspect a connection between the teacher's death and the accident this weekend. When, or if they made that connection, Janet was sure to get a visit.

Janet had barely gotten a bite of her sandwich when the ringing doorbell nearly made her choke on it. 'Shit,' she thought. She waved to Kimberly meaning the child should finish eating while she rose to answer the door. If it was the police already, she didn't know what she would do. Janet was relieved to find Dr. Satish on the other side of the door. He was a couple of hours earlier than promised, but still a welcome sight.

After he apologized for not calling, he asked Janet about Krystal. He was particularly interested in how she had reacted the other day. Kimberly heard his voice from the kitchen and entered the living room just as her mother and the doctor were making their way to Krystal's bedroom. Once there, the doctor took out his stethoscope and checked Krystal's heart rate and breathing rhythm. Satisfied that everything was normal, he turned back to Janet.

"You said she reacted to you with facial twitches and by closing her hand," he said, putting his equipment back in the bag.

"Yes," Janet said. "I was just talking to her and then her lip quirked. I don't remember how many times before she just held my hand."

"Do you remember what you were talking about?" Dr. Satish asked.

"Not really," Janet lied. "I was just talking and I can't remember about what, but I got so excited I think I just kept babbling."

"Hmm," he said. "Well, let me take a look at the readings from that day and we-. What's wrong?" He stopped his original line of thought when he noticed the pained look on Janet's face.

"I was so excited when it happened," she explained. "I didn't think to print the EEG."

Dr. Satish grimaced and looked at the machine that was connected to the little girl's head. The Electroencephalograph, or

EEG, monitored the impulses from the brain that would tell them if she began experiencing 'normal' brain activity. It wouldn't guarantee them that she was coming out of the coma, but it would alert them that changes were happening and they would be able to give her an MRI to be more certain of her changing condition. Unfortunately, the results had to be documented before the doctor could authorize an MRI for the insurance company to pay for it.

"Okay," he said after giving it some thought. "What we can do is keep monitoring her. I can come by two or three times a week, just in case, and hope for another reaction."

While the doctor was talking, Kimberly had an idea and moved to the other side of her sister's bed. She climbed up beside Krystal, lowered her head and cupped her hand between her mouth and Krystal's ear. It took less than a minute of Kimberly's whispering before Dr. Satish and Janet noticed a twitch at the corner of her sister's mouth. Doctor Satish's mouth fell open in astonishment and he reached over to press the button on the machine that would print the EEG readings. He nodded to Kimberly to continue whispering to her sister and she complied.

For ten whole minutes, Kimberly whispered with no results until suddenly, her sister's lip twitched again, and then again. The facial tics continued for a few seconds before her mouth settled into a serene smile.

"Amazing," Dr. Satish said.

Kimberly continued whispering to her sister for a few more minutes with no further results. Doctor Satish turned off the printer, tore off the printout, and began studying it. After a moment, he looked up at Kimberly. "If you don't mind, what were you saying to her?" he asked.

Kimberly smiled and said, "Just sharing sister secrets."

The doctor shared her smile and took a seat in the chair by Krystal's bed. He thought for a moment before continuing. "I understand the need for sisters to have their secrets," he began. "But it's important to know what exactly you were saying. It may be the key to helping Kryssi wake up."

Kimberly took hold of Krystal's hand and concentrated on their joining while she spoke. "I was just telling her about school," she all but whispered. "I was telling her what was happening in class and what I was doing to get extra points. And then I told her what we could do together when she woke up." Kimberly looked up at the doctor, saw his smile and returned it shyly.

"I think that is a super way to get Kryssi excited about coming back," he said. He looked to Janet and continued to smile. "With your permission, I will schedule an MRI for Kryssi on Friday." Receiving a tearful nod, he stood and continued. "Just keep talking to her about the future and telling her about what is going on in your lives. Don't forget to print the EEG readings when she responds."

"We will," Janet promised.

Kimberly laid her head beside her sister's and watched as the doctor continued his examination. After checking her feeding tube and catheter, he put all of his equipment back in his bag and stood looking at the sisters.

"It's amazing," he said. "Now that she's gotten some color back in her, you could almost swear she's about to wake up any second."

"She will," Janet said with a smile. She saw the doctor to the door and returned to find the sisters still lying together. "You should finish eating," she said and eventually led Kimberly back to the kitchen where their sandwiches waited.

It was Friday morning, or at least he thought it was, when Jason opened his eyes and looked around. The house was a mess. The living room floor was littered with beer bottles and some stench was coming from the kitchen that he couldn't identify. He rolled off the sofa and landed on something hard with sharp edges. He rose up just enough to fish out the offending object. When he saw what it was, tears formed in his eyes and blurred his vision.

The toy he landed on was the same toy JJ had been playing with when he came home last Friday. The boy dropped it on the floor when he found out they would be getting pizza for dinner. Jason rolled over, hugged the small truck to his chest, and wept. He lay there thinking about his son and all the time he spent not being a father to the boy.

The images of JJ kept being blurred by visions of Billy crying much the same way Jason was now doing. The words he spat at his brother began ringing through his own head, causing him to close his eyes and cover his ears in agony.

With his son's image and his own words screaming through his mind, he got up and stumbled to the front door and out to Billy's truck. Without even looking behind him, he backed out into the street and sped away in search of something to quiet his pain. He drove to the bar he had practically been living in all week. When he tried to enter, he found the door locked and began kicking it. When he had kicked out his frustration, he slumped next to the still locked door and continued crying.

Jason was still sitting beside the bar door when the owner showed up an hour later. He had cried himself dry, but JJ's face and his own voice combined with Billy's still circled his mind, taunting him mercilessly.

"Man, it is way too early for you to start drinkin'," the bar owner said as he unlocked the door.

"Didn' ask yer 'pinion," Jason said as he followed the man inside.

Jason was drunk in less than twenty minutes, and the wary bartender began serving him water instead of whiskey, hoping he wouldn't have to call the police... or an ambulance. He caught himself slipping off the stool a couple of times before deciding to take his drink to one of the booths. For the next couple of hours, he sat there staring at his shot glass, and wondered what in the hell happened that night. He knew for a fact that Billy drove like an old woman. He would never blow a red light. 'What the hell happened?' he asked himself. He looked at his shot class and realized that it was just water. He pushed it away and got unsteadily to his feet.

The bartender met him before he got to the door and asked him if he wanted a cab. Jason just shouldered past the man and dug his keys from his pocket. He decided to get the answers he wanted from the one person that had them.

~*~

She paced the living room floor wondering what her next move should be. The plan was so easy to make, now that she knew the nightmares wouldn't haunt her. The problem came with deciding the order of their deaths. 'Who is next?' she asked herself, taking a seat on the sofa. Her new plan called for Jason to be last. She wanted him to suffer before killing him. The death of the little boy meant nothing to her in the end. He was just an extension of his father, and her new perception meant that every part of the man should die. She considered going after his daughter next. It would be easy. She's probably grieving over her brother and wouldn't be as cautious as normal.

'No,' she thought. 'I need to finish with the brother first.' With that in mind, she opened the laptop and went to her favorite search site. She started by researching hospital security and protocols for getting into and out of the intensive care unit, where she learned Bill McDowell was. Once she got this information, she began looking into ways people have died in the hospital.

She found what she wanted rather quickly, now that she was learning precisely what to look for. Now all she had to do was get everything ready. Before logging off the internet, she checked one more site to see if she could find any information on the McDowell boy. Nowhere on the internet did she find any mention of the wreck and the boy's death. Satisfied that she had gotten away with it, she once again scrubbed her browser history and closed the laptop. She needed to gather some supplies and then make her plans for Billy McDowell.

~*~

SEVEN

"Kimberly," Janet said as she walked through the living room, putting her earrings on. She went into Krystal's room knowing that's where she would find her other daughter as well. "Grandma will be here in a few minutes. She's going to watch the two of you while I run out for a while."

Kimberly looked up from her book and saw her mother dressed in a pair of blue jeans and a t-shirt she'd never seen before. The girl was surprised since she couldn't remember ever seeing her mother in anything but business attire and classy casual clothes. The little girl didn't think there was a t-shirt in the house, especially since she was the one who preferred to dress down and even she didn't own one.

"Where are you going?" the little girl asked.

"Mommy just needs to run out and pick some stuff up before we take Kryssi to get her MRI," Janet answered. "I won't be gone long."

Kimberly nodded and returned to her book, only to look up again a few minutes later when her grandmother arrived. She waited while her grandmother checked on Krystal and left the room, before returning to her book. When she heard the doorbell a few minutes later, she figured that Dr. Satish had decided to come by early. She went to the living room to find her grandmother already answering the door.

Kimberly had no idea what to do. It wasn't Dr. Satish on her front porch. It was Mindy McDowell. She realized the girl had no idea who they were, but coming to her house like this was a huge risk. If her mother had been home… Kimberly didn't want to think about what would have happened.

"Oh, Kimmy," her grandma said as she turned and saw her. "You have a visitor."

"Hey," Kimberly said as the older woman allowed Mindy to enter. "Are you okay?" Mindy nodded as she came into the living room. "I heard about JJ," Kimberly continued. "I didn't know your number, but I sent you an email."

"I don't have a computer," Mindy said. "I can only check it when I'm at school or Lesley's."

"Oh," Kimberly said, not knowing what else to say.

"Can we just talk for a little bit?" Mindy asked. Kimberly really wanted the girl out of the house before her mother returned, but she felt it would probably be helpful to talk to the girl for a while.

Kimberly thought quickly. She wasn't about to take Mindy into Kryssi's room. The living room and kitchen were a bad idea in case her mother came home and saw Mindy here. A thought occurred to her. "Grandma, we're going up to my room to talk for a while," she said.

"Go ahead, Kimmy," Jean said. "I'll fix you some sandwiches real quick." The two girls went upstairs to Kimberly's room and closed the door.

"I thought you hated being called anything but Kimberly,"

Mindy said as the two of the sat on the bed.

"I do," Kimberly answered. "I think she does it to bug me." Kimberly could see the other girl wanted to talk. She could also see that the girl didn't know where to start. "How is your uncle?"

"He still ain't awake yet," Mindy said. "They still got him in ICU."

"What's that?" Kimberly asked, already knowing the answer, but trying to make the other girl feel more at ease.

"It's where they keep you if you're so bad off they don't know if you're gonna make it or not."

"Oh."

"They said he's got a bunch of broke bones and his brain's swelled up."

"How are your mom and dad?"

"Mom cries all the time. Dad's been drunk since it happened." Mindy looked down at her hands. "I'm not comin' back to school for a while."

Kimberly understood how the girl felt. When her dad died and Kryssi went into the coma, she felt much the same way. For her though, school was a blessed escape. She threw herself into her books and didn't look back. She reached out to take hold of Mindy's hand and watched as the girl began crying. Kimberly let her cry until she was ready to go on.

The girls spent over an hour upstairs in Kimberly's room. After Kimberly's grandmother brought their sandwiches and sodas up, Mindy told her friend all about her little brother. She told her how much she was going to miss him. She talked about how important her aunt and uncle were to her. Every so often, she would stop and ask Kimberly why this had to happen to them. Kimberly couldn't give her the answer. When she had finally talked about her family enough, she asked Kimberly about her family.

Kimberly told the girl as much as she could without revealing to the girl the truth about her father and sister. She mostly told her about her and her mother's lives over the past three years, not even mentioning her father and Krystal. When she ran out of things to say, she offered to let Mindy use their computer to talk to Lesley and Kelly.

Kimberly ran downstairs to grab the laptop and brought it back up to her room. Mindy sent quick emails to the other girls and waited for them to reply. While they waited, Kimberly showed Mindy what she had done for their project and promised her friend that she would be able to turn it in alone if she didn't come back to school in time. After Mindy got her responses from Lesley and Kelly, the two of them went back downstairs.

"Thanks for letting me talk for a while," Mindy said as the reached the bottom of the stairs. "Mom's really not in shape to talk and Daddy's not an option."

"Who do we have here?" Janet asked. Kimberly froze in place.

"Hi, Mrs. Tucker," Mindy said.

"M-M-Mom, this is Mindy," Kimberly stuttered. "Remember I told you about her?"

"Yes, I remember," Janet said, with her smile plastered on her face. She wanted to scream, 'What the hell is she doing here?' but chose to ask, "What brings you here, Mindy?"

"I just wanted to talk to someone," the dark haired girl said. "Kimberly's closer to my house than Lesley, so I came over and…"

"I see," Janet said, letting out a breath she didn't realize she was holding. It made sense that the girl would want someone to talk to after everything she had experienced. "Well, has Kimberly offered you anything to drink?"

"Yes, ma'am," Mindy said. "Thank you."

"Mom, I hope you don't mind," Kimberly said handing the laptop over to her mother. "I let Mindy use the laptop to send a couple of emails to Lesley and Kelly. They hadn't heard from her and they were worried."

"It's quite alright," Janet said. 'No it's not!' her mind screamed. "Well, I'll just let the two of you talk. Kimberly, don't forget we have to get going in a little bit."

"Okay," Kimberly said.

"No, I have to get back home," Mindy interrupted. "Mom's at home by herself, and I don't want her to be alone when Dad gets home."

"Call me if you need anything," Kimberly said as she walked her friend to the door. Once she saw Mindy out and past the driveway, she closed the door and turned to face her mother. "I can explain," she said.

~*~

Janet and Kimberly watched as the first images of Krystal's brain came onto the monitors. Neither of them understood what they were seeing, but both were worried. Each knew the secret of what made Krystal react to them, but neither wanted the other to know. The doctors told them that they could talk to Krystal through the microphone to try to get her to respond while in the MRI, but neither of them wanted anyone else to know what they said to her. Dr. Satish encouraged them to say anything to Krystal to get a response from her. Kimberly approached the microphone and leaned in.

"Kryssi," she began. "We had company today. I don't know if you noticed, but Grandma came by and spent some time with us. I think we can talk her into taking us to the zoo when you wake up." There was no response from the child inside the machine. The technician watched the monitors for any changes in the girl's synapses. "And my friend Mindy came by to see me." A large area of the brain on the monitor suddenly glowed red.

"We have something," the technician said.

"Go on, Kimberly," Dr. Satish encouraged.

"She was a little sad," Kimberly said into the microphone. "But after we emailed Lesley and Kelly, she felt a little better." Kimberly noticed the technician and Dr. Satish nodding while continuing to stare at the monitors. "When you wake up, I'll introduce you to all of them."

At that, the monitors lit up like Christmas trees and Dr. Satish's head snapped up. "She's seizing!" he shouted as he ran from the room. The technician began pressing a series of buttons and the images left the monitors as the huge machine in the next room slowly eased the convulsing girl back out.

"What's happening?" Janet asked the technician.

"She's having a seizure," he answered.

"Why?"

"I'm not a doctor, ma'am," he said as he watched nurses and interns flood the room on the other side of the glass. "I couldn't hazard a guess."

Janet and Kimberly watched in horror as the professionals in the next room began working with Krystal, trying to get her past the seizure. A nurse came into the control room and ushered them out to a waiting area. She assured them that someone would be out to give them some answers soon. Janet and Kimberly waited for twenty minutes before Dr. Satish came out smiling.

"This is amazing," he said. "The seizure seems to have reset Krystal's brain in some way."

"Please tell me what's happening," Janet said, the panic still coursing through her.

Doctor Satish sighed and shook his head before beginning. "The nearest we can figure is that whatever Kimberly was saying to Krystal gave her enough motivation to fight to come back. When she started reacting to Kimberly, her brain began sending signals to every part of her body. That's what caused the seizure."

"So she's waking up?" Janet asked hope blooming in her eyes.

"She's not awake yet," the doctor said, holding up his hands.

"That may still take some time. Nevertheless, her brain is more active than it has been in the past three years. It is still below normal, but it is steady."

"Can we see her now?" Janet asked.

"Not just yet," the doctor said. "We're still running some tests. Give us an hour and she'll be in her room." Dr. Satish held Janet's arms. "This is very good news," he said.

Janet sat down in the chair as the doctor turned to walk back into the main area of the hospital. Tears began rolling down her cheeks and a smile slowly crept onto her face. Kimberly sat beside her mother and placed a hand on her arm. Janet thought about having both of her daughters home and healthy once again and new tears formed. She thought about how scared she had been just a few minutes ago and everything that happened in that room. She remembered Kimberly talking just before Krystal started to seize. Remembering what Kimberly was saying, reminded Janet of something.

"Sweetie, I need to go use the bathroom," she said as she opened her purse. "You go grab us some snacks."

"Okay, Mommy," Kimberly said as she took the money her mother handed her before they headed their separate ways.

She walked straight to the elevator and it opened immediately when she pressed the call button. The car took her up two floors, where the intensive care unit sat. She walked down the hall past the each open door and looked in. Up ahead she saw a maintenance technician on a ladder. It looked like he was repairing or installing something. As she got closer, she saw that he was disconnecting what looked like a camera. Her pulse picked up as she looked at the ceiling behind her. She saw another small dome, like the one lying on the top of the maintenance guy's ladder, back past the elevator she just left.

She turned back and continued down the hall. The maintenance guy was absorbed in examining the camera and paid her no attention. Further down the hall stood the nurses desk, unmanned. She looked in the room just past the ladder and saw something that brought her up short. Sitting in a chair beside the bed was a sleeping Jason McDowell. 'This is it,' she thought. She slipped into the room quietly.

As she crept over to the bed, she watched McDowell continue to snore. The smell of alcohol was so strong it was making her sick from the other side of the bed. She examined the man lying on the bed. She traced the tube coming out of his mouth and the line that led from the IV bag to his wrist. She looked at the wires that ran from his chest to the monitors. Finally, she looked around and saw a box hanging on the wall. A small tube stuck out of the top of it and she went over to examine it.

The tube was a syringe that a careless nurse had put in the box without making sure it went all the way in. She reached over and grabbed a pair of small gloves from a cardboard box mounted to the wall by the door. Once she had them on, she pulled the syringe from the box and looked it over carefully. It looked like the syringe had threads, which someone would screw on a needle. She looked back at the man lying on the bed and noticed the IV line had a branch on it to allow her to screw on such a syringe. She grabbed another glove from the box and pulled the plunger from the syringe.

She crept back to the bed and screwed the syringe into the IV line. Once it was secured, she bit a hole into a finger of the spare glove and slipped it over the end of the syringe. She took a deep breath and lowered her lips to the line. She blew as hard and long as she could into the IV line, until she saw all of the fluid had passed through it. She quickly unscrewed the syringe and removed her gloves, putting them all in her pocket. She heard the machine start to beep faster and crept back out of the room, looking to make sure the nurse's station was still empty.

She went toward it planning to circle around so she wouldn't pass the maintenance man again. She made it around to the other side of the ward and to the elevator on that wall unseen. Once in the elevator, she pressed the button to go down one floor. Once she got off, she circled back around to her original elevator to go back down.

~*~

Shane Morrow sighed as he sat at the desk and logged into the system. It had been a long and boring shift and now he was going to unwind before he clocked out for the day. Once he was signed in, he brought up the Billy and Joyce McDowell accident files. He noticed that the crime lab had their results in. He found what he was looking for immediately, but the results were negative. All brake lines were full of fluid and the pads were brand new. The rotors were in good shape and showed little wear despite the truck's age. Results on engine testing were still pending.

'Well, that answers that,' he thought as he closed the files. Something still bothered him about the accidents so he opened up a search for Billy McDowell in the criminal justice system. He found the man's name listed on a case from three years ago. Apparently, Billy had posted bail for his brother. He didn't think it would lead to anything, but curiosity made Shane open the case file.

As he read the complaint, and then opened the attached incident reports, Shane Morrow began to get a sick feeling. He saw a name he recognized in the reports. Three years earlier, Jason McDowell was arrested for running down a man and his daughter. According to the transcripts, he was acquitted of vehicular homicide and reckless endangerment. When he read the name of the victims, he knew right away that there was more to this case than he suspected.

Shane logged out of the system and went to the locker room to change into his civilian clothes. Once he was dressed and had his off-duty weapon secured, he clocked out and headed for his personal vehicle. He sat in the car for a few minutes thinking about Jason McDowell and his arrest three years earlier. 'John Tucker's daughter was at the house the day Joyce McDowell died.' Shane thought. Hiss problem with that thought was that he doubted the girl could arrange to make the McDowell woman fall from the roof. 'Her mother on the other hand…' Shane started his car and left the police parking lot. Instead of heading home, he drove in the opposite direction. There was something, which he needed to look at for himself.

~*~

The alarms sounded suddenly and scared Jason out of his slumber. He looked over at his brother and then to the monitors beside him. Before he could register what was happening, the room filled with people. One grabbed his arm and pulled him from the room asking him what had happened.

"I dunno," he slurred as he stumbled out of the room. He watched as the people in the room worked furiously over Billy and wondered, himself, what had happened.

"Coming through!" someone shouted. Jason barely got out of the way when an orderly ran into the room pushing a cart. Some of the doctors and nurses moved out of the way to make room for the equipment. Jason watched his brother lift off the bed when the doctor shocked him with the paddles.

It took them ten minutes to decide the fight was over. One of the nurses left the room and went to the desk at the end of the hall. He saw her pick up the phone before his attention was drawn back to his brother's room. The doctors and nurses began filing out of the room. One of the doctors stopped and looked at him.

"Mister McDowell?" the doctor asked.

"Yeah," Jason said.

"I'm sorry. Your brother didn't make it."

"What happened?" Jason asked. The doctor looked up as another person joined them. Jason looked at the security guard and then back at the doctor. "What's goin' on?"

"Mister McDowell, we need to know what happened in there," the doctor said.

"So do I," Jason spat.

"Your brother was still critical, but stable," the doctor said. "His shouldn't have died that suddenly."

"The hell you sayin'?" Jason exclaimed.

"Pending an autopsy, I'm afraid I have to list your brother's death as unknown and suspicious," the doctor said. "Mister McDowell, this is Officer Wallace," he continued, introducing the guard. "He will stay with you until someone comes back to speak with you."

"The hell he will," Jason said as he turned to leave.

"Mister McDowell," the guard called. "If you try to leave I will subdue and restrain you."

Jason turned and looked at the guard menacingly. "You'll do what?" he asked.

"I will shoot you with a Taser," the guard smiled. "Then I will handcuff you to a part of this building that will still be standing when the world comes to an end."

Jason gave the guard a hard look before changing directions. "Somebody better figure out what the hell's goin' on here," he said as he walked past the doctor and the guard. He heard one of them walking behind him, but didn't bother looking behind. He figured it was the guard. When he got to the nurse's desk, he asked for the waiting room. He looked back at the guard who nodded, then headed in the direction the nurse indicated.

~*~

Shane turned onto Main Street and headed towards the railroad crossing. He wanted to take a closer look at the crash site before he went to poke around the McDowell house. As he came up on the intersection where the accident occurred, he pulled to the side of the road and killed the engine. Before he could get out of the car, however, his cellphone rang.

"Morrow," he said after connecting the call.

"Shane, I got news for ya," Keith Rogan's voice came from the other end.

"What's up?"

"The McDowell guy from the wreck last week just died." Rogan said.

"Huh," Morrow said. "Well, they said he was still touch and go, right?"

"Yeah, but the hospital just called the station. They said the guy was critical but stable. They're saying suspicious until further notice."

"Really," Shane said. "Who caught the case?"

"I'm meeting Parris there."

"I'm on my way," Shane said as he snapped his phone closed. He started his engine and put his strobe light on his dash before pulling out.

Ten minutes later, Shane Morrow was walking the halls of Piedmont Memorial Hospital. He made his way to the ICU ward and saw Keith standing with one of the hospital security guards.

"Hey," he said as he approached. "So, what's going on with the McDowell death?"

"Docs told me to keep that guy under guard until you guys got here," the guard said pointing to the man sitting in a chair close by.

"Why?"

Wallace shrugged his shoulders and said, "They said his brother's death was suspicious and he was the only one in there. Detective Parris is interviewing the doctors now."

Shane nodded and looked up to the ceiling and noticed a camera bubble just a couple of doors down from the room Billy McDowell had been in. "What about video footage?" he asked.

"The camera was down for maintenance for about an hour," Wallace said. "They already interviewed the maintenance guy. He said no one came past him while he was here. None of the nurses saw anyone else either."

"So that's Jason McDowell," Shane said.

"You know the guy?" Rogan asked.

"I just read about him," Shane answered, looking at McDowell with keen interest.

Rogan watched Shane with a small smile. He knew that Shane wanted to interview the guy in the chair. He also knew that Parris would have a stroke if he did. Shane wasn't about to break protocol, especially off-duty, but Rogan was picking up a vibe that made him think that Shane had a few questions for the guy that the detective wouldn't think of. The three officers just stood there taking turns watching the suspect while they waited for the detective to arrive.

~*~

Janet tossed the chip bag into the trashcan and took another sip of her soda. It had taken her longer to get back than she had thought, but she wasn't surprised to see that Kimberly had waited for her to return before enjoying her own snacks. She was halfway through with her drink when she saw Dr. Satish rounding the corner.

"Doctor," she greeted, meeting him halfway. "How is she?"

"She's fine," the doctor said. "In fact she's better than fine."

"You mean she's-"

"No," Dr. Satish said, interrupting her. "She's still not awake yet, but her neural activity is increasing by the minute. I want to keep her here tonight and maybe tomorrow in case she wakes up."

"You think she might after all this time?"

"It's looking that way," the doctor said. "I wouldn't be surprised at this point. I'll take you to her." Doctor Satish led Janet and Kimberly to Krystal's room while explaining what he thought had happened to the little girl. As he spoke, he became more and more excited. "It's just that this rarely happens and we still have no idea exactly what the changes mean or why they are happening now," he said as they got on the elevator.

By the time the three of them entered Krystal's room, Janet and

Kimberly were more confused than ever before. All that mattered to the two of them was that Krystal was getting better. They stood over the little girl and watched as she continued to sleep. Kimberly was the first to notice the movement.

"What's wrong with her eyes?" she asked.

"That's REM," Dr. Satish said in amazement.

"Rem?" Kimberly asked.

Doctor Satish looked at her and nodded as he pulled a pen light from his pocket. "Rapid Eye Movement," he said. "It means she's dreaming."

"She can dream in a coma?" Janet asked.

"Maybe," the doctor said. "But it would be very unusual for her to experience REM state in her condition." Janet and Kimberly did not have to be medical experts to know that this was a good sign. The doctor pulled out his cellphone and spoke quickly and quietly. Soon several other doctors were in the room as well. Some were looking over Krystal's monitors while some were trying to get reactions from her by poking, prodding and tweaking different parts of her. Kimberly jumped slightly when she saw her sister's foot jerk when a doctor poked it with a pin.

Mother and daughter stood back quietly while the doctors continued their series of reaction tests. By the time they were finished, every doctor in the room was excited by the results. They all began discussing the case, leaving the room and a thoroughly confused Janet and Kimberly behind. Janet moved to follow them and called out for Dr. Satish. The doctor paused at the door and looked back.

"Mrs. Tucker," he said. "You saw it. She's reacting to stimuli."

"She's..." Janet couldn't say it again. She didn't want him to correct her and tell her she was mistaken.

"She's coming back," the doctor said. "Maybe not tonight or tomorrow, but she is definitely coming back."

Angela sat on the sofa whimpering. Her tears had dried up days ago and it seemed she had no more fluid left to release. Even without the tears, she cried. She cried when she awoke and all day until the sleep medication the doctors prescribed made her sleep. Mindy made sure her mother ate and took the medicine each day. She'd even helped her mother bathe, as the woman seemed unable to perform even this simple task.

Angela was so wrapped up in the loss of her son that she began shutting out the world. A couple of her co-workers had stopped by every day since the accident. Two of them worked on her behalf to arrange JJ's funeral, through which Angela barely survived. Jason practically had to carry her away from the grave as the boy's coffin was lowered.

Today was one of her good days and she was aware when Mindy helped her to the sofa and fixed her some breakfast before leaving the house. Angela hadn't noticed when her daughter got home until the girl helped her to the bathroom. She stayed on the sofa and refused the soup the girl brought her a couple of hours ago. Angela heard the phone ring, but didn't bother getting up.

"Mom," Mindy said to her a few minutes later. "Mommy, you have to go upstairs and get dressed." Angela looked at her daughter in confusion. "The police just called," Mindy continued. "They need you to come to the hospital and pick up Daddy."

"Dad-" Angela began. "Wha-?"

"Mommy," Mindy said again after a couple of minutes. "Did you hear me?"

"Yes," Angela said. "Your dad's in the hospital."

"No, Mom, he's at the hospital."

"Billy?"

"No, Mom," Mindy said. "Come on, get dressed. We have to go."

Mindy looked at her mother for a moment and realized the woman was not thinking clearly. She had never seen her mother like this and it scared her. She needed to find a way to get her mother to focus, so they could go get her dad. The ten-year-old considered shaking her mother but figured that would be useless. As she stood there thinking, a scene from a movie she had seen during the summer came back to her.

In the movie, a man was trying to get his hysterical wife to pay attention to something, but the woman wouldn't listen. Suddenly the guy slapped her across the face and she started to calm down. Mindy remembered that the woman wasn't too happy to have been slapped and had slapped her husband back, but the girl figured that if she could get her mother to pay attention, it would be worth it.

She leaned down, kissed her mother on the cheek, and

whispered, "I'm sorry," before leaning back and raising her hand. The sting she felt in her hand was nothing compared to the ache she felt in her chest. Tears formed in her eyes as her mother stared at her.

"Why did you do that?" Angela asked.

"I'm sorry, Mommy," Mindy bawled. "I needed you to listen, but you couldn't."

Angela brought her hand up to her cheek and Mindy saw her own hand printed in red on her mother's face. As the child cried harder, Angela stood up and grabbed her by the shoulders. Her own tears chose to return, and through them, she looked at her daughter. "I am going to say this once," she said. "You do NOT hit anyone ever again."

"I'm sorry, Mommy," the girl repeated and continued crying.

"Now what is so important that you decided to act like your father?" Angela demanded.

Mindy looked up and through her sniffling, she said. "Th- the hospital called. Th-they s-s-said you needed to come pick Daddy up. Th-they said he's drunk and they w-won't let him drive."

The focus of Angela's anger switched from her daughter to her husband. 'As if I don't have enough to worry about,' she thought. That thought, however, brought her mind back to her son and the knowledge that she would never see or hold him again. She pictured JJ in his shorts and t-shirt that he wore when he went out the door with his uncle that night. As a fresh wave of grief came over her, Angela felt her arm being shaken.

She barely heard Mindy's voice as the little girl said, "Mommy, please get dressed." The words did get through to her, and she looked at her little girl. She lost her son a week ago, but it was only beginning to dawn on her that Mindy had lost her brother, too. Angela still had a child that needed her, but this past week, that child had been the mother. Angela shook herself. She couldn't get past the loss of JJ. She doubted she ever would, but she had to be stronger than she had been for Mindy.

"Okay, baby," she said as she stood up. "You have been so helpful this week. I'm sorry I put all that on you." Tears fell heavily from her eyes as she bent to hug her daughter. "I'm gonna try to do better. But, just in case, I need you to help keep me focused. Okay?" Mindy nodded as tears fell from her own eyes. "Just, um, find a way that doesn't involve slapping Mommy." Mindy let out a choking half sob, half laugh as she and her mother hugged.

Angela called for a taxi and went upstairs to get dressed while they waited for it to arrive. Ten minutes later, she and Mindy got into the back seat of a yellow Crown Victoria and headed for the hospital.

~*~

EIGHT

Dr. Satish shook his head. He had watched Krystal's reactions improve for the past three days, but the girl still refused to wake up. It was her last barrier before rejoining the world, and it frustrated him as much as it did her family that she had not yet breached it. As he made a few notations on her chart, he turned back to Janet and sighed.

"There is nothing more we can do, here," he said. "I think since she began responding at home, that may be the best environment for her complete recovery."

"What about her medical attention?" Janet asked.

"I will stop by every evening and check in on her," Dr. Satish answered. "Trust me, she'll be safe."

Janet nodded thoughtfully. She and Kimberly had been very excited the past few days. From the moment Krystal started responding to other stimuli, both of them started breathing sighs of relief. Janet considered sharing her secrets with Kimberly as she had Krystal, but decided against it when it occurred to her that Krystal likely had no memory of the secrets.

Doctor Satish excused himself to begin Krystal's discharge. Janet sat on the edge of the bed and took her daughter's hand. "We'll go home and get you comfortable," she said. "Then after you rest a bit, you can wake up and we'll get to do what we should have been doing all along." Janet felt the child's fingers tighten around her own and smiled. "It won't be long now," she said.

For her part, Kimberly's excitement over her sister's recovery was tempered by the fact that her mother still made certain she went to school, today. Although happy not to miss school, Kimberly still worried that Kryssi might wake before she got out. She wanted so much to be the first face her sister saw when she finally woke.

The girl fidgeted in her seat all day. Even while spending time with Kelly and trying to coax a word or two from her, she constantly thought about her sister and wondered if she was waking at that particular moment. By recess, she was ready to spring for the door. Her first stop was the principal's office to see if her mother had called.

"Miss Tucker, I promise to come get you the moment your mother calls," the secretary said. "Now, go enjoy recess." Kimberly went to recess, but her mind was occupied. Today, she didn't spend as much time talking with her friend as usual, but Kelly didn't seem to mind. The two walked hand-in-hand around the playground silently, just waiting for the bell to ring to call them back to class.

By the end of the day, Kimberly was on edge and couldn't wait to leave school. It wasn't until she was stepping onto the school bus that it occurred to her that she was actually eager to leave school for the first time in her life. She barely noticed when the bus left the school, and didn't even acknowledge when they stopped at Kelly's house and the girl left. She was, in fact, so lost in thoughts of what was happening at the hospital, she didn't realize she was in front of her own house until the bus driver called her name.

"Tucker!" the driver called. "Are you going home today?"

"Yes, ma'am," Kimberly said, shaking her head and grabbing her book bag. She was almost to her porch before she noticed her mother's car parked in the driveway. Kimberly bolted for the porch and barreled through the front door.

"Whoa," her mom said as she ran through the living room. "Close the door first, and then go see your sister."

"She's home?" Kimberly asked.

"Door," Janet said pointing towards the portal. "And yes, she's home." Once she made sure Kimberly shut the door, Janet continued into the den turned bedroom to sit and wait for her daughter to wake. Kimberly was right behind her and Janet decided to let the girl greet her sister before making her go get the snack she had laid out. Less than a minute later, the girl and snack were back in the room sitting at the table. Soon, Janet was on her laptop while Kimberly began studying.

She slipped out of the house at just after midnight. It was a miracle considering she had to sneak out of Krystal's room without waking... Well, she just couldn't think of that now. She made it out of the house and headed east. It took her a while to find the bottle in the basement, but she was glad that she hadn't gotten rid of it yet.

As she came up on the house on Willowood Drive, she noticed

that only the old Buick was in the driveway. She quietly made her way to the driveway and laid the bottle on the pavement. 'That's that,' she thought as she pulled the pliers from her pocket. 'Now, I just need to find some place to put these.' She went to the front porch and peer through the darkened window. When she didn't see anyone in the living room, she tried the doorknob and was shocked when the door actually opened.

As she stumbled through the dark hall into the living room, she considered turning on a light, but since she didn't know if anyone was in the house, she decided not to risk it. A few steps into the living room, her foot hit something and the clink of glass bottles nearly caused her to jump out of her skin. She took a deep breath to calm herself and the smell of stale beer nearly caused her to gag. She held a hand out and took another tentative step before she touched something soft.

Patting her hand across, she realized she was feeling the back of a chair. The feel and sound of bottles on the floor combined with the smell of alcohol convinced her that this must be Jason's usual seat. She bent over and placed the pliers in the corner of the chair, beside the seat cushion. That accomplished, she began feeling bolder and turned back to the hall. She felt her way to the staircase and carefully ascended the stairs.

She knew who her next target was, but she still didn't have a clue about what she was going to do. She opened the first door and found that the light coming through the open window somewhat a blessing. She looked around the room at an unmade bed and dresser with nothing on it. A picture of a little boy lay on one of the pillows. It was a picture of the son, the one she killed a couple of weeks earlier.

Finding nothing of interest, she went back to the hall and opened the next door. This was obviously Mindy's room. The posters on the walls clearly illustrated the tastes of a young girl. Her hand brushed against something and she looked down at the dresser top. The girl's schoolbooks were piled on the dresser. She scanned the spines of the books until she saw the spring-like binding of the girl's notebook.

She pulled the notebook out, noting its original location. She had barely begun leafing through the notebook before she found a post-it note with some writing on it. She took the notebook over to the window so she could make out the writing on the note. Her eyes widened as she realized she had the girl's login information for the school's server.

She tucked the note into her pocket and replaced the notebook. Quietly, she made her way back down the stairs and to the front door. She had just grabbed the doorknob when she saw a set of headlights turn into the driveway. She moved quickly back into the living room and began picking her way through it. Moving to where she hoped the back of the house was. She found the door to the kitchen by accident and almost immediately bumped into the table.

She could hear voices coming towards the house and felt her way around the table and to the back wall. Finally making it to the back door, she opened it at the very moment someone opened the front door. She slipped outside and quietly closed the door as a light came on in the living room.

She managed to slip around the house without being seen or heard and paused to peer around the corner. Seeing no one at the window or on the porch, she moved quickly for the sidewalk, noting as she passed the driveway that the bottle she brought had been crushed, presumably under someone's foot.

Once on the sidewalk, she nonchalantly walked past the house and down the block before making her way back home via the same route she had used before. This time, she didn't miss her own house when she came into the back yard. She slipped back into the house and was down in the basement in under a minute. Once she was back in her nightclothes, she dug the post-it note out of her pocket and stuffed the clothes back under the shelf.

After returning to the main floor, she took a moment to hide the note before returning to Krystal's room and resuming her previous resting place. Five minutes later, with plans and ideas swimming through her head, she fell asleep.

~*~

Shane Morrow turned onto Willowood Drive, heading for Billy McDowell's house. He couldn't help himself, something about these accidents kept gnawing at him. Every piece of evidence said they were just that, accidents, but he couldn't fight the feeling that there was something more. Billy McDowell's death was what cemented it for him. Detective Parris got a judge to order a rush on

McDowell's autopsy, but nothing came from it. The ME, ruled the death a result of the accident, but it just didn't make sense. How could a man just die when the doctors said he was stable? Wouldn't he show some indication of decline beforehand?

These thoughts rambled through Shane's mind as he drove down the street, until he came to a stop in front of the McDowell's house. After parking on the street in front of the house, he took a moment to look over the front yard and driveway. Getting out of his vehicle, he gave the neighborhood a quick scan and opted to lock his door, just in case. He walked through what passed for grass in the yard and stepped onto the front porch before knocking. When the little girl answered the door, he recognized her from the day he came to this house for Joyce McDowell's accident.

"Hi," he said. "I'm Officer Morrow. Is your father at home?"

"Dad!" the girl called, leaning back into the house. "The police are here to see you!"

"What the hell for now!" Jason called from inside the house.

"Come on in," the girl said as she stepped back to allow Shane to enter. As he stepped across the threshold, the smell of alcohol nearly knocked him back out the door. Mindy led him to the living room where her father sat nursing a beer.

"Mister McDowell," Shane said as he came around to the front of the chair. "I'm Shane Morrow. We met at the hospital the other day."

"Go ahead and sit down," Jason said. "Yer blockin' Sports Center."

Shane sat on the edge of the sofa and took out his notepad. "Mr. McDowell," he said again, when he had gotten as comfortable as possible. "I came by today to talk to you about your brother."

Jason looked at him with a cross between contempt and malice. "If you ain't gonna tell me what the hell happened to him, I ain't got nothin to say."

Shane was ready for some resistance. He had gotten permission to release the details of the autopsy from Detective Parris, who had closed the file since the autopsy couldn't prove foul play. "According to the autopsy, it looks like your brother died as a result of his injuries," he told Jason.

"So why's the police still botherin' with it?"

This is where Shane began getting into the murky area of his visit. He intentionally came here out of uniform because this wasn't an official investigation. Since the accidents weren't being investigated, department policy prevented him from representing himself as an officer when looking into them. To Jason he said, "I just have a few things I wanted to follow up on." Jason snorted and took another drink of his beer. "As you know, your brother had his accident just a couple of weeks after your sister-in-law fell to her death."

"So," Jason said as he turned up the volume on the TV.

"So, I was just wondering if it is coincidence, or if they are connected." Jason gave the officer a hard look. Shane went on quickly asking, "Mr. McDowell, when was the last time you checked the brakes and fluid on your truck?"

"I just put new brakes on it last month," Jason snapped. "You ain't gonna say it was bad brakes on the truck that caused it."

"No, sir," Shane said holding up a hand. "We found the brakes were brand new. What about the fluid, did you fill it up when you changed the brakes?"

"Didn't have to," Jason said. "There was enough in it."

"Do you remember how much?"

"Almost full," Jason said. He was starting to get annoyed with the man sitting on his sofa. "Look, I fixed the brakes myself. They ain't what caused the wreck."

"What did?" Shane asked, hoping it was a sudden enough swerve to catch him off guard.

"How the hell should I know?" Jason snapped. "I wasn't in the damned truck! Maybe you should ask the no-drivin' son-of-a-bitch that wrecked it!"

Shane sighed. He looked at Jason for a few seconds before venturing his next question. "Do you know of anyone who would have something against Billy and his wife?"

"Nope," Jason said turning back to the TV.

"How about against you?"

"Like who?" Jason asked.

"Anyone you might have made angry. Have you made any enemies in the past couple of years?"

"Nope," Jason said. "'less you count the assholes that fired me."

"What about the Tuckers?"

Jason looked at the man, confusion written all over his face.

"Who?" he asked.

"John Tucker's family."

"Who's that?"

"You killed him three years ago when you drove through Dugan's Bakery," Shane said, not bothering to hide the disgust he felt. 'How can you forget about killing someone?' he thought.

"Oh," Jason said leaning back in the chair. "Hell, I don't even know if they're still in town. Last time I seen any of 'em, they was cryin' in the halls when I left the courthouse."

Shane looked at him for another few seconds, trying to decide if he should let him know that John Tucker's daughter was in this very house less than two months ago. He decided against it. There was no telling if the man would react. If he did, it could cause trouble where none was needed. Instead, he decided to end the conversation and maybe poke around a bit. "Do you mind if I take a look at the roof where your sister-in-law fell? Maybe look at the Buick?"

"Min!" Jason shouted. The girl who opened the door came back into the living room promptly. "Show him how to get on the roof."

"It's upstairs," Mindy said turning towards the hall. Shane got up to follow her and paused with his hand out to Jason.

"Thank you for your time, Mr. McDowell," he said.

"Yeah," Jason said taking another drink from his beer. When he didn't take the officer's hand, Shane dropped it and followed Mindy upstairs. At the top of the steps, Mindy opened the first door and waved him in. She pointed to the window at the front of the house and said, "She probably went out her window, since it's closest to the dish."

"The satellite?" Shane asked.

"Yeah." She watched as Shane climbed out the window and then followed him.

"You shouldn't be out here," Shane told her. "It's not safe."

"I'm okay," she said. "I come out here all the time." While Shane looked around the dish mounting, Mindy thought about what she had overheard downstairs. "That man you were talking about, that my dad killed, was he Kimberly's dad?"

Shane looked back to her and kneeled down. "Your parents haven't talked to you about that have they?" he asked. Mindy shook her head. "I don't think I should either," he said. "Maybe you should talk to your mom about it."

"I overheard her and Aunt Joyce talkin' one day," Mindy said. "I didn't know it was Kimberly's dad that he killed." As Shane continued examining the roof, something occurred to her. "Do you think she knows?"

Shane stopped a moment and thought. "I can't imagine she doesn't," he said.

"I wonder why she never said anything."

"Maybe she realized you didn't know and didn't want to upset you," Shane said. "Or maybe she realizes that you're not responsible for what your dad did and just wants to be your friend." Something caught his eye and he bent down to pick up a nail. The spike of the roofing nail was a dark rusty color. 'That could be blood,' he thought. He pulled a plastic bag out of his pocket and dropped the nail in. "How often did your aunt come out here?" he asked as he straightened up to look over the edge.

"Every couple of weeks," Mindy said. "One of us was always havin' to come up to fix the dish." Shane nodded and indicated that it was time for them to go back inside the house. Once they were back downstairs, he thanked her for her help and gave her his card, making her promise to call him or have her parents call if they thought of anything that might help.

Once outside, he went over to the Buick and looked over the hood. He could see the dents where Joyce's body warped the metal and blood was still present on some of the pieces of glass. He took out another plastic bag and dropped a few pieces of the bloody glass into it. As he started down the driveway, he saw a half-crushed soda bottle lying on the ground. The liquid inside it looked nothing like soda, however, so he bent to pick it up. He sniffed at the opening and wrinkled his nose. 'That's a hell of a coincidence,' he thought as he pulled out yet another bag.

Once he had the bottle bagged, he gave the driveway another good look and then headed for his own car. He sat in it and thought about everything for a few minutes. 'Is it possible that someone is targeting the McDowell family members?' he thought. 'Could the Tucker woman be capable of it?' He didn't have those answers, but he did have something that could point to foul play. He started his car and turned it towards the station. It was time to visit Ben at the Crime Lab again.

~*~

Janet hung her coat on the peg in her office. After almost a month of being back at work, she was finally starting to get back into her old routine. She sat at her desk and got ready to sort through the material purchases for the company's current projects. Part of her job was to make sure the materials met with government guidelines for safety. Once she checked the material specifications against government requirements, she went over the amount of the materials that was purchased. Everything was well within the approved parameters, so she approved the purchases and arranged to pay for them. Next, she opened her email and scanned through the new messages until she came to one from Chrystal.

Opening it, she learned that the head of Human Resources was leaving the company and Chrystal wanted to know if Janet wanted the new position. She forwarded the salary information along with the responsibilities of the position. Janet printed the email and took the copy upstairs to the HR office. She entered the office and was greeted by a young girl, who looked young enough to still be in high school.

"Are you, Melissa?" Janet asked as she checked the email to make sure of the name.

The girl looked up at her and smiled. "Yes," she said. "You must be Janet Tucker."

"Yes," Janet said, assuming Chrystal had already told the girl that she'd be interested in the position. "I just came up to find out if the position was really available."

"Well, it will be in a couple of weeks," Melissa said, as she tucked a lock of her short brown hair behind her ear. "I enlisted in the Air Force a few months ago and I ship out to Basic Training at the end of the month."

"Oh," Janet said, surprised, "Congratulations."

"Thanks," Melissa said. "I wasn't sure they'd take me, but it looks like I'm just barely in the age range."

"That's lucky," Janet said as she took a seat across from the girl. "When did you turn eighteen?"

Melissa sat and looked at her for about a half a minute before a smile spread across her face. "About nine years ago," she said.

Janet's jaw dropped. "Honey, I'm so sorry," she said. "I thought you were still in high school."

Melissa let out a quick laugh. "No, thank God," she said. "I hated high school. I didn't really enjoy school at all until I got to college."

The two women talked briefly about their college experiences and Melissa's plans for her Air Force career before getting down to why Janet was there. It took Melissa just a half an hour to show Janet how to use the HR system. Greenholdt's Human Resources Department not only managed employee scheduling, payroll and insurance, but public relations as well. Janet also learned that HR managed the legal team and made sure all contracts were in order.

"So if you take the job, my last two weeks will basically be showing you how to keep everything running smoothly," Melissa said as she began pulling out some paperwork. "Now, the problem with being HR director is that you have no control over your own pay. Chrystal handles your scheduling and pay, but you still get to handle your own insurance."

"Makes sense," Janet said. "It just keeps HR honest."

"Exactly," Melissa said with a smile. "Now, all I need you to do is fill out this paperwork, I'll send it to Chrystal and once she and Mr. Greenholdt approve it, the job is yours."

"Ok," Janet said, and began filling out the forms. She finished quickly and handed them back to Melissa, who stood and beckoned Janet to follow. A few seconds later, they were outside of Chrystal's office, waiting for her secretary to finish a phone call.

"Hey, Mel," the secretary said when she hung up the phone.

"Hi, Gina," Melissa said. "Is Chrystal busy?"

"She's just talking to Marvin about Mrs. Tucker," Gina said. "Go on in."

As the two women entered the office, Chrystal and an older man looked up, both with smiles on their faces.

"So, you found a replacement?" the man asked.

"Yes," Melissa answered. "Daddy, you remember Janet Tucker. Janet, Marvin Greenholdt."

"Daddy?" Janet asked in surprise.

"Just Marvin will do," Mr. Greenholdt said with a laugh.

"No, I mean..." Janet paused trying to figure out what to say that wouldn't embarrass her or anyone else in the room.

"Don't pay any attention to him," Melissa said. "He's spent so much time around the construction sites that he's forgotten that he's not as funny as he thinks he is."

"So, you're taking the job?" Chrystal said, coming to Janet's rescue.

"Yes," Melissa answered for her handing over the paperwork. "Pending your approval."

"Marvin," Chrystal said.

"Chrystal swears you're the right person," Marvin said. "She's never been wrong yet." Janet smiled as she watched her friend approve her promotion. "Now, let's talk about my raise," Mr. Greenholdt continued, smiling.

"See," Melissa said. "Nowhere near as funny as he thinks."

Janet couldn't help but laugh. She just got a promotion within weeks of coming back to work. This should go a long way towards helping her stay out of financial jeopardy.

After being congratulated by her bosses, Janet followed Melissa back down to the Human Resources office, where the woman began talking her through the process of managing the employee portfolios.

"Now, since this is Wednesday, we're going to go ahead and start processing paychecks so they'll be ready for Friday." Melissa was explaining as Janet brought up the appropriate screen. "Oh, here's something you might have to work with occasionally. This guy here is out for FMLA." Janet looked at the name Melissa pointed to and her blood ran cold. "His wife called it in a couple of weeks ago. His brother died... Are you okay?" Melissa saw the look of horror on Janet's face and touched her shoulder to get her attention.

"I didn't know he worked here," Janet said, her breath coming short.

"This guy?" Melissa asked. "Do you know him?" Janet couldn't speak. She just nodded. "How do you know him?" Melissa asked. Janet couldn't answer. She jumped up from her chair and ran from the office.

Janet barely made it to the bathroom stall before she started throwing up. No matter what her plans were for McDowell, she never thought she would end up working for the same company as him. The thought that she was so close to him, literally made her ill. It took her a few moments to get control of her stomach. When she was finished, she was only mildly aware enough to be happy she hadn't made a mess. She shakily got to her feet and flushed the remains of her breakfast down the toilet before exiting the stall. As Janet made her way to the sink, Chrystal came into the bathroom, a worried look on her face.

"Janet, I'm so sorry," she said. "I had no idea he was working here. I just sent a notice to his supervisor."

"How did I end up working at the same company as him?" Janet said as tears formed in her eyes.

"I'm sorry, honey," Chrystal said. "It's entirely my fault. If I had thought to do a personnel check…"

"No," Janet said, wiping her eyes. "You can't do a personnel check every time you hire someone, just in case their husband's killer might be working here."

"Still, I sent the notice to his supervisor. He's gone now."

"You can't," Janet said, suddenly looking up. "He's out on FMLA."

"Family and Medical Leave Act doesn't technically cover an employee being out for the death of a child," Chrystal said. "When his wife called it in, she told us that her son had been in an accident. His supervisor noted he was very upset, but didn't realize the child had died."

"But-"

"Company policy gives parents a week off for the death of an immediate family member," Chrystal continued, avoiding Janet's protests. "He's been out two weeks. We're covered, and he's fired." Janet was at a loss for words. She looked at her friend and new tears formed. Chrystal brought her into a hug and comforted her while the woman wept in relief.

Jason sat in the recliner drinking. He searched the satellite channels but couldn't find any sports worth watching. He settled on the Outdoor Channel and sat back watching a group of guys hunting deer. 'I can do this,' he thought as he watched the older man with the beard raise his rifle. 'All they're doin' is sittin' there waitin' for somethin' to come to them.' Just as the old man fired his gun, the telephone rang. Jason muted the TV and picked up the receiver. "What," he growled into the receiver.

"McDowell," the man on the other end of the line said. "It's Kevin from Greenholdt."

"What," Jason repeated with less irritation in his voice.

"Listen man, we just got word from the main office," Kevin said. "They gave you a week off for your kid's funeral but you were supposed to be back last week. They told me I had to let you go."

"Let me go?" Jason yelled as he jumped to his feet. "What the hell? I thought I could have up to twelve weeks."

"Apparently not," Kevin said calmly.

"This is bullshit man," Jason said. "I been doin' good work for that company, and they fire me 'cause I took a couple weeks off for my dead boy?"

"Look man, if you got a grievance, you need to take it up with HR. I just got the message to let you go."

"Fuck them," Jason spat into the phone. "Maybe they'll change their minds when I sue the shit out of 'em." As he slammed the phone down, he threw his nearly empty bottle at the wall and was only slightly gratified when the glass shattered and flew everywhere. He plopped down in the recliner and felt something poke his thigh. He reached into the side of the cushion and pulled out a pair of pliers. 'The hell did these come from?' he asked himself before tossing them onto the end table.

She stepped quietly into the den-turned-bedroom and walked over to the bed. She checked to make sure they were alone. Krystal lay on her bed and a look of concentration came across her sleeping face. She knew the girl was dreaming again. She didn't want to let anyone know what she had done, or what she was about to do, but this was probably her last chance to share her secret before it was all over.

She sat on the bed, leaned close to Krystal's ear, and began whispering, "I just have two more to kill before I take care of Jason. He's going to be last, and he's going to suffer the most."

She smiled when the girl's features smoothed. As she took Krystal's hand in her own, she whispered a promise that soon, everything will be made right. Krystal's hand tightened on hers and she lifted it to place a soft kiss on it.

~*~

"Angela," Barry Swenson called as she made her way to the break room.

'God,' she thought. "Yes," she said aloud as she turned to face him.

"Listen, our sales are way down this quarter," he manager began. "We're going to have to make some cutbacks."

"Barry, I can't take another reduction in hours," Angela said. "I'm barely getting by as it is."

"Listen, I'm not talking about decreasing your hours."

"Then what?"

"I hate to do this, but we need to let you go."

"What?" Angela asked. "Why me? Why not one of the new hires?"

"It's about dedication," Barry said, clearly not wanting to give her his reasons. "You've missed work a total of eighteen days in the past two months."

"Barry, there have been deaths in my family," Angela said hotly. "My sister-in-law, my son and my brother-in-law have all died in the past couple of months."

"And I sympathize with you," Barry said. "But to be honest, you only really needed to miss work for your son's funeral."

"Are you shitting me?" she asked. A sudden calm came over her. "Are you really trying to pull this bullshit with me?"

"Angela, you need to calm down," Barry said taking a step back. "Just accept this as part of business and I'll personally write you a recommendation."

Angela gritted her teeth and seethed. "I recommend you stick it up your ass," she growled as she pushed past him and headed for the exit.

"I'll remember this attitude when I get a reference call," he called after her.

As much as she wanted to turn around and punch the little twerp, Angela kept walking towards the exit. Once outside she made her way to Billy's truck and got in. She sat behind the wheel crying for a solid ten minutes before pulling herself together. As she started the car, she decided she would look for another job tomorrow. 'And I'll be damned if I put this shithole on my resume,' she thought as she pulled out of the parking lot.

Janet pulled the trashcan to the curb and fastened the bungee cord around the post to make sure it didn't fall over in the wind.

She looked up as the light blue Prius pulled up and parked at the curb in front of her house. She stood there as she watched the handsome young man get out and walk around the car.

"Missus Tucker," the young man said as he walked up to her.

"Yes," Janet said and then recognized the young man. "Oh, Officer…" She couldn't quite remember his name.

"Morrow, ma'am."

"Yes, Officer Morrow," Janet said. "I didn't recognize you out of uniform."

Shane looked down at his polo shirt and khakis before looking up again and smiling. "I suppose so," he said. "I came by today, hoping to talk to you."

"To me?" Janet asked.

"Yes, ma'am" he said. "I was wondering…" he paused to search for the proper approach, before blurting out, "Do you happen to know Jason McDowell?"

Janet was shocked. She looked at the young officer as if he had spat on her. After a moment, she replied, "You obviously know I do. He killed my husband and left my daughter in a coma."

Shane nodded and lowered his eyes for a moment before continuing, "Are you aware that it was his sister-in-law whose death your daughter witnessed?"

"I found out the next morning when I read the paper," Janet said. "I had a talk with Kimberly. She hasn't been back since."

"What about you ma'am?" Shane asked.

"What about me?"

"Have you been to the McDowell residence?" he asked.

Janet's heart started pounding. 'Does he know?' she asked herself. She let annoyance show on her face. "Officer Morrow," she began, "I have worked hard keeping as much distance between myself and the McDowell family as I could."

"Do you know anything about brakes?" Shane asked quickly.

"Brakes?" Janet repeated.

"Car brakes."

"No," she said, now more confused than angry. "My father has to remind me when I need to get my car serviced. John used to be the one to take care of all of that. I'm afraid I never did get around to figuring it out."

Shane watched her face carefully as she answered. 'If she's lying, she's good at it,' he thought. "Do you know anyone else who might have a grudge against the McDowell family?" he asked.

"Officer Morrow," Janet said. "As I have told you, I have worked very hard to stay away from the McDowell family. Except for Kimberly being in his daughter's class, and me finding out he worked for the same company as I do, I haven't had any contact with them since he got away with killing my husband."

"Jason McDowell works for the same company as you?" Shane asked.

"Not anymore," she answered in a clinical tone. "He was terminated this morning for violating the company's attendance policy."

"You are aware that he just lost his son and brother," Shane said.

"The company gave him a week off to grieve for his son," Janet said. "He decided to take two."

"Did you have something to do with his termination?" Shane asked.

"I didn't ask them to fire him, no. However, when the vice president learned that he was working there, she decided to enforce the attendance policy herself and terminated him."

Shane nodded and made a note on his pad. "What is the vice president's name?" he asked.

"Chrystal Adams at Greenholdt Construction," Janet answered. "Her decision was backed by Marvin Greenholdt, CEO and president."

"Okay," Shane said pulling a card from his pocket and handing it to her. "I know it's not likely, but if you see the McDowell family or hear of anything relating to them, could you give me a call?"

Janet took the card and leveled a gaze at him. "Officer Morrow, I assure you that I have no intention of knowing anything more about that family. If I had my way, I would never have heard of them in the first place."

Shane gave her a curt nod before turning to his car. After he got in, he put his notepad in the passenger seat and buckled his seatbelt. As he pulled from the curb, he shook his head thinking that things could have gone better with Mrs. Tucker.

~*~

Janet went back inside the house and placed the card on the end table, next to the front door. She heard something on the stairs and looked up to see Kimberly coming down. "Hey," she said. "Finished with your homework?"

"Yeah," Kimberly answered as she joined her mother at the foot of the stairs. "What time's dinner?"

"About an hour," Janet said.

"Can we have-" Kimberly was interrupted by a series of loud beeps coming from the den. She and her mother both looked that way a brief second before bolting towards the sounds. They had barely gotten into the room before they both stopped short. Krystal was on her bed... sitting up. She looked at her mother and sister and a smile showed on her face. "Hi, Mommy," she said.

Janet's heart burst with joy and tears flowed freely down her face, as she and Kimberly rushed to Krystal's side. "Oh, baby, you're awake!" Janet cried as she ran to the bed and threw her arms around the girl.

Kimberly was smiling and crying at the same time. She joined her mother in embracing her sister. "I can't believe it!" she said as she cried on Krystal's shoulder. The three of them held onto each other for a few long minutes.

Krystal opened her eyes, shifted them from Kimberly to her mother, and whispered, "I missed you so much. I tried to tell you I was okay." This only got her held tighter by her mother and sister.

~*~

NINE

"I have to call Dr. Satish," Janet said. "I can't believe you're awake!" she placed a hand on each side of Krystal's face and leaned in to kiss her for what seemed the hundredth time.

"Can't it wait, Mom," Kimberly asked as Janet got off the bed.

"Honey, he needs to know," Janet said. "It's important for her recovery."

"Can't we put it off for a little while?" Kimberly asked. "I just want to enjoy this before everyone starts poking and prodding her."

"I don't think I want them poking me either, Mommy," Krystal said.

Janet looked at her two girls. Logically, she knew she should call the doctor. How could she deny these two angels when she only just got the one back? Janet thought for a minute before coming to a conclusion. "How about if I call him and make sure he understands that we won't go in for an examination for at least a couple of days?" she asked.

"But he'll still want to come by," Kimberly said.

"Maybe, but we'll just tell him we want a little time alone." Janet answered. "But I do want to call Grandma and Grandpa."

"Can't they wait too?"

"No, Kimberly."

"But, Mom," Kimberly whined. "I just want it to be us for a

little while. I like us being together while it's quiet."

"Please, Mommy" Krystal pleaded.

Janet looked at her girls and her resolve melted. "A visit from Dr. Satish," she said. "And then a day or two just the three of us." Janet went out to the living room to make her call.

"You know about Daddy, don't you," Kimberly said when her mother left the room. Krystal lowered her head and nodded. "I'm so sorry, Kryssi. I should have been there with you."

"Mommy needed you here while I was asleep," Kryssi said, shaking her head. "If Daddy hadn't pushed me out of the way…" Krystal couldn't finish. The memory of that day was quite vivid. For her, that day was just as clear as yesterday was for her mother and sister. Kimberly leaned in to hug her sister once more.

"I wish it had never happened," Kimberly whispered. "But everything's going to be okay now that you're back."

A few moments later, Janet returned to Krystal's bedroom. "Doctor Satish will be here in a couple of hours," she said to the girls. "And I have called Chrystal and got myself the rest of the week off. I'll call tomorrow and get you out of school tomorrow and Friday," she said to Kimberly.

Kimberly was torn by this news. On the one hand she wanted desperately to spend time with her sister before everyone started coming by, but she had also never missed more than a couple of days of school in her life. She looked at her sister and a smile spread across her lips. 'It's not like I'm falling behind,' she thought. 'And if I'm going to miss, this is definitely a good reason.'

Janet sat on the end of the bed and smiled at her two daughters, who were now snuggled together. She noticed how they kept mirroring each other's moves, just as they did in the years before the accident. A thought suddenly occurred to Janet and she adopted a frightened look before saying, "Oh no."

"What?" Krystal asked.

"I'm going to have to figure out how to tell you two apart all over again," Janet said and then laughed at her daughters' reactions. The twins joined her laughter and hugged each other tighter. As Krystal leaned into the hug, she felt a slight pull at her stomach and looked down.

"When does this come out?" she asked.

"We'll ask Dr. Satish when he comes," Janet said. The three of them sat and talked about things that had happened since the day of the accident. They were having so much fun being caught up. It occurred to Janet that she just might not answer the door when the doctor came.

~*~

She opened the door for the doctor and showed him into Krystal's room. She smiled at his shocked expression and let him get to his task of checking the girl over. While he was busy, she slipped into the living room and retrieved the note from its hiding place. She sat on the sofa and opened the laptop. She found the student login for the grade school and signed in with Mindy McDowell's credentials. Scrolling through some of the links, she clicked on the student email link and started a new message. After sending her message, she started to log out of the system when a thought struck her. She quickly began a new message and typed furiously.

She looked up and saw the doctor talking to Krystal, probably asking her how she felt and what she remembered. When she sent her second message, she looked at the inbox and saw she already had a response from her first message. She closed the laptop and stood to put the note back in its hiding place before returning to Krystal's room.

Shane was about to log out of the system, after filing his end of shift report, when he noticed a new email in his inbox. He opened the message without even looking at the sender. As he read the message, his eyes widened. 'No way,' he thought. He printed the message and took the hard copy upstairs to the detective bureau.

Once he entered the detective's bullpen, he scanned the room until he found the one he was looking for. Detective Parris was sitting at his desk going through a thick folder, when Shane approached.

"Detective," Shane said when he got to the desk. "Do you have a minute?"

"Officer Morrow," Parris said. "What can I do for you?"

"I wanted to talk to you about the McDowell case."

"I don't have a McDowell case," Parris said.

"Billy McDowell," Shane said. "He died in the hospital the

other day. You interviewed his brother because the death was suspicious."

"That file is closed," Parris said, finally looking up from his folder. "The M.E. determined that he died from his injuries."

"I don't think he did," Shane said, handing the email to the detective.

"What's this?"

"I got that a few minutes ago," Shane said, taking a seat across the desk from the detective. Parris glanced at Shane and raised an eyebrow before reading the email.

"Dear Officer Morrow," he began, "I wanted to let you know that I think my daddy killed my uncle Billy and my brother. He was 'workin' on his truck just before he told Billy to drive his truck. Daddy never like Billy or Joyce and I know he was fighting him the day after aunt Joyce died. You half, spelled 'h-a-l-f' to do somthin, 's-o-m-t-h-i-n' to stop him before he kills me or Mommy. Mindy McDowell" Parris handed the paper back to Shane and sighed. "Well, the spelling and grammar suggests a kid wrote it," he said. "Could be she did something to get punished, and she's just trying to get even with her dad."

"Or she could just be telling us that her dad killed his brother and son," Shane said.

"Why would a father kill his own son?" Parris asked.

"Come on, Detective," Shane said. "You know as well as I do, parents kill their kids, sometimes for no reason whatsoever." Parris scoffed and Shane continued. "Of course, maybe he didn't plan to kill his son. He might not have realized that his brother was taking the kid."

"Maybe, maybe, maybe," Parris said. "It's supposition without proof." Shane just sat there and stared at the man. "Look," Parris said. "If you really think there's something to this, go interview the father, talk to the girl. If you get me something solid, I'll take it to the captain and get the case reopened."

"Something solid," Shane said as he stood up.

"It's called evidence," Parris said. "If you want to make detective, you have to know stuff like that." Shane folded the email and put it in his pocket before turning to leave. "And make sure you do it on your own time!" Parris called after him. "It's not an active investigation!"

Shane left the detective bureau in a huff. This is just the sort of thing that irritated him the most. Shane knew when something wasn't right. This part of being a patrol officer irritated him the most. He was a ten-year veteran patrol officer and he knew when something wasn't right. However, anytime he tried to explain a gut instinct to a detective, he was shot down.

Sometimes it seemed that explaining instincts to a detective was like explaining nuclear physics to a toddler. All they wanted was evidence. It's all anyone wanted since those shows started. They wanted the science, but they seemed to forget that it was the hunches that pointed them to the science. Shane fumed over this line of thought while he changed into his civilian clothes. After clocking out, he went down to the crime lab to look for Ben.

The leader of the CSI team was sitting in his office when he saw Shane enter the lab. "Officer Morrow," he called, waving Shane in. "I was about to call you. We got back the results on that evidence you brought in."

"Great," Shane said. "What did you find?"

"Well, first the nail," Ben said, pulling a sheet of paper from a folder. "It definitely had Joyce McDowell's blood on it. According to the autopsy, she had a small puncture on the bottom of her right foot, which would indicate that she had stepped on the nail just before falling from the roof."

"Okay," Shane said.

"And the glass is from the same windshield as the specimens we collected the day of the incident. Her blood was on it and no one else's." Ben said.

"What about the bottle?" Shane asked.

"That was an interesting piece of evidence," Ben said, pulling out another piece of paper. "We compared it to the fluid we drained from McDowell's brake lines. It matched perfectly."

"So it was the same type," Shane said.

"No," Ben said. "It was the same fluid. The fluid we drained wasn't much degraded from what was in the bottle. We found traces amounts of brake dust in the truck lines as were in the bottle."

"So the fluid had to have been in the bottle just before the wreck," Shane surmised.

"Exactly," Ben said. "I would say no more than a day or two, but likely more recent."

"How long would it take a drained line to refill?" Shane asked.

"On that truck, about thirteen to fifteen compressions," Ben said with a thought.

"He'd have to pump the brakes about fifteen times?"

"About that," Ben said, leaning back in his chair.

"So, based on the witness statements about how he was driving, he could have been struggling with the brakes before he entered that intersection," Shane said.

"Yes," Ben said and then leaned forward. "And the amount of fluid missing from the truck would be just slightly more than the four lines would hold."

"Were there any prints on the bottle?"

"No," Ben said, "Which is what bothers me." Seeing Shane's expression, he explained, "Someone who bothered to drain the brake fluid and leave the bottle lying around, surely wouldn't have worn gloves or wiped his prints from the bottle."

"I've seen people do dumber things."

"Me, too. Especially lately," Ben said.

"In your opinion, could the accident have been a homicide?"

"In my opinion, any homicide could be made to look like an accident," Ben said. "But the wreck is starting to look intentional."

"Do you have enough to get the case re-opened?"

"No," Ben said. "I hate to say it, but the bottle is inadmissible."

"What?" Shane asked. "I had the owner's permission to-"

"In spite of that," Ben said, holding up a hand. "You brought me the evidence in a zippered plastic sandwich bag. Although I don't doubt your integrity, there is still a chain of evidence issue, and with the rules of evidence being what they are, I'm afraid I can't use it."

"So why did you run the tests?" Shane asked.

"I was curious."

Shane rubbed his temple a second before asking his next question. "Where do we go now?"

"I don't know about you," Ben said, "But I'm going home. However, the next time you find evidence, call me. I can come by, collect it and make sure the integrity of the evidence is intact."

After leaving the crime lab, Jason went down to his Prius and decided to go, again, to the scene of Billy McDowell's accident. Afterwards he was going to talk to Jason McDowell, again. Something was going on with this case, and it was bugging him that he kept slamming into walls.

~*~

"I am telling you, Mrs. Tucker, we need to get her to the hospital and have her examined," Dr. Satish was saying. "I just want to make sure there are no long term effects on her."

"Doctor, look at her," Janet said. "She's awake, she's happy, she's active. She even remembers everything from that day."

"I understand that, Mrs. Tucker," Dr. Satish said. "But there are so many things to consider. Not just her memory, but her ability to learn new things, her mobility, even her diet."

"About that," Janet said. "She's wanted pizza since she woke up…"

"No," Dr. Satish said. "While she still has the G-tube in, I don't want her eating anything by mouth except soft foods."

"About that," Janet said. "When can she get the tube out?"

"Let's get her examined first," Dr. Satish said.

Janet groaned in frustration before going back into Krystal's room. The girls were sitting on the bed talking, but they looked up when they saw their mother standing in the door.

"What's wrong," Kimberly asked, recognizing her mother's annoyed expression.

"Doctor Satish insists on taking Krystal in for a full examination," Janet said.

"But, Mommy, you promised!" Krystal whined.

"I know, baby," Janet said. "But we have to get you looked at if you want that tube out."

"Why can't it wait until tomorrow?" Krystal asked.

"You need to be examined to make sure there are no-"

"What difference will one day make?" Kimberly asked, interrupting the doctor.

"When it comes to brain injuries and comas, even a minute could make all the difference in the world," Dr. Satish said.

"Why don't I just bring her in tomorrow morning?" Janet asked.

"I'm sorry, Mrs. Tucker," the doctor said. "This is very important. I have to insist we take her to get an MRI and make sure she can sustain her health if we decide to remove her tube."

Janet and the girls tried in vain to convince the doctor to let them have a day or two to themselves before subjecting Krystal to a series of examinations. Finally, Janet gave up and agreed to take Krystal to the hospital. Kimberly volunteered to stay behind and get her room ready for her sister to join her. With a resigned sigh, Janet called her mother to watch Kimberly. She had to tell her mother about Krystal waking up, which meant that no matter what time they got home, there would be a house full of Tuckers and Greens waiting on them.

The ambulance arrived before Jean and Adam did, but only by a minute or two. By the time Krystal got into the ambulance, her grandmother had hugged and kissed her no less than a dozen times. The woman watched as the ambulance pulled away, followed by Janet's blue Taurus. Soon more vehicles arrived. John's parents, David and Carol, and his brother Mike arrived a few minutes after the ambulance left. Sue and her husband Bob followed quickly.

In no time, Kimberly found herself playing host to her entire family. She spent almost an hour answering their questions. They wanted to know when Krystal woke up and what her first words were. She told them how Krystal looked and what she knew about what they could expect. Sometimes, being the smartest eight-year-old in the family was a chore, especially when she had other things to do.

With her Grandma Jean's help, she made sure everyone had a drink and a sandwich before heading upstairs to get her room ready to have a roommate. She listened for a moment as the adults laughed and celebrated the miracle of her sister's return. Soon, she had the second bed made, half of the closet cleared, and several drawers emptied. When she looked at her accomplishment, she realized that she had nothing to put into the closet or the drawers. She knew she had to do something about this quickly, so she went downstairs to talk to her Grandma Jean.

~*~

"Mommy," Krystal said. "Do I have to wear this gown home?"

"Oh, sweetheart," Janet said. "I didn't even think when we left the house. I should have gotten you some of Kimberly's things. I'll run down to the gift shop and pick you up something."

"I'm afraid the gift shop is closed," the nurse who was taking Krystal's vitals said.

"How long will these exams take?" Janet asked.

The nurse brought Krystal's file up on the monitor of the portable computer. She looked at the doctor's orders and said, "They have her scheduled for an MRI and a stress test. Then they are going to give her something to eat and see if it will stay down. If it does, they'll schedule her to have her tube removed." She shook her head. "Those and the other tests they have, will have her busy for at least six or seven hours."

"Six or seven hours," Krystal said, with a groan. "Mommy, this isn't fair."

"It has to be done, Kryssi," Janet said. "The sooner it is, then the sooner we can get back home, so everyone can start spoiling you."

A knock on the door interrupted the conversation. "Excuse me," the tall dark-skinned man said. "My name is Jeff, and I have a date with a Miss Krystal Lynn Tucker, for an MRI."

"This is she," Janet said, pointing to Krystal.

"Can you tell me her birthday just to be sure?"

"June 25, 2005," Janet answered.

"Okay then," Jeff said. "Are you ready, Miss Tucker?"

"No," Krystal said with a pout.

"Will you go anyway?"

"Yes," she said, her pout deepening.

As Jeff wheeled the gurney out of the room, Janet turned to the nurse. "I'm going to run out to get her some new clothes," she said. "Can you let her know I'll be right back?"

"Of course," the nurse said.

Janet made her way out of the hospital and to her car. She left the parking lot and headed to the shops in town. She knew they would still be open since none of them closed before dark during the summer.

~*~

Mindy walked into the living room and took in the scene. Her dad was in the recliner drinking and watching TV. Her mom was lying on the sofa. Angela held a cigarette was still burning, with a long stack of ash still attached. Mindy went over to the sofa and gently pulled the cigarette from her mother's fingers. She wasn't surprised to find the woman asleep. It was the new normal in this house.

She looked in the kitchen with a little despair. She figured that she would eventually have to clean the kitchen herself, or no one would do it. That, however, could wait. She needed to get some food in the house first. She turned to her father and looked at him with disgust.

"I need to get us some food," she said, swallowing her distaste for him.

"Go on then," Jason said.

"I need some money," she said.

"How did I know that?" he asked. He pulled out a few bills from his pocket and handed it to her.

"What am I gonna get with five dollars?" she asked him.

"It's all I got," he said. "Check that suitcase yer mom's always draggin' with her."

Mindy sighed with contempt and went upstairs to her parents' bedroom. She spotted her mother's purse on the bed and opened it. After digging through the contents, she found her mother's wallet and pulled out forty dollars. She thought for a moment, and pulled out another ten, just in case.

After calling a taxi, Mindy ran to her own room to change clothes and make a quick shopping list. A few minutes later, she stepped outside when she heard the taxi driver honk his horn.

"I need to get to Wilder's on Second," she said.

"Eight-fifty," the driver said. "No offense, but I've had too many kids try to get a free ride from me." The driver held out his hand, and Mindy handed him ten dollars. When she received her change, the driver put the car in gear and she was on her way.

~*~

"Oh there you are, Kimberly," Grandma Carol said, as Kimberly descended the stairs. "Where have you been off to?"

"I was just upstairs getting our room ready for Kryssi," Kimberly said.

"You must be so excited to have her back in your room with you," Aunt Sue said.

"Yeah, but I have a problem," Kimberly said.

"What is it?" Grandma Carol asked.

"Well, Mom donated all of Kryssi's clothes when she realized we had out grown them," Kimberly said. "The problem is, Kryssi would never like wearing any of the clothes I like, so…"

"Do you want to get her some new clothes?" Grandpa Adam asked.

"Yes, please," Kimberly said. The adults started clamoring, each pulling out their wallets or grabbing a purse. After they counted the collection, Kimberly saw that her grandparents, aunt and uncles had donated almost $250 to get Krystal some new clothes.

"This is great," Kimberly said. Then with a mischievous smile, she asked, "Can I borrow your car, Grandpa?" The whole family laughed at this and Adam held out his keys. Stunned, Kimberly reached for them, only to have him pull them back.

"Only if I can drive it," he said.

"Don't be silly," Grandma Jean said. "What do you know about buying girls clothes, or your own for that matter." Adam enjoyed the round of laughter at his expense as his wife took his keys from him. "We'll be back when we're broke," she said as she and Kimberly left the house.

Soon, Jean and Kimberly were driving along Second Avenue heading to the middle of town, where Kimberly's favorite shops stood. The girl fidgeted in her seat as they drove. This was the first time in her life that she was actually looking forward to shopping. To be honest, if she wasn't going for Krystal, she would have stayed at home, reading a book. 'I can't believe she's really awake,' she thought. 'I need to find her something special to celebrate her coming back.'

She stepped into the store and looked around slowly. She knew she had to go to the girl's clothing department, but she just liked the atmosphere in this store so much. After having a quick glance, she headed back to the area that held the girl's sizes. She had only went a few feet when she stopped to look at a collection of shirts, she was sure her mother would love.

'I'm going to need to come back here with Mom,' she thought. She had just picked up a shirt and started looking at it, when something at the front of the store caught her eye. She looked that way and saw a yellow taxi stop at the curb. Just as she was about to return to the shirt, she saw Mindy McDowell getting out of the taxi alone.

She looked around quickly to make sure no one saw her and then she slipped out of the store, shirt still in hand, to follow the girl. After watching the girl window shop for a minute, she had a decent idea of which way Mindy would go. She slipped down an alley to the back of the stores and ran ahead to the next alley. She finally noticed that she still had the shirt in her hand and a thought occurred to her. After slipping the shirt over her own clothes, she quietly came halfway through the alley. She searched the alley and found a broken beer bottle, with sharp points on the end. She ducked behind a dumpster and waited, watching the other end from the corner of the dumpster.

Sure enough, she saw Mindy come into view a moment later. She leaned back a little, but kept an eye on her target. When Mindy was halfway past the alley, she cried out for help. She saw Mindy stop and look, so she cried out again. The girl took a tentative step into the alley. She moaned as if in pain and saw Mindy come closer. "Please help me," she whined.

Mindy began running toward her. As soon as she saw the girl get close enough, she sprang from behind the dumpster and thrust the broken end of the bottle into the front of the girl's neck. Before Mindy's eyes widened in surprise, she pulled the bottle out of the girl's throat, dragging it sideways before stabbing it into the side of the child's neck.

She ran to the back of the alley, removing the new shirt as she went. She wrapped the bottle into the shirt and ran to the end of the block. She rubbed the bottle through the shirt, hoping that she removed her fingerprints, and then threw the entire package into the closest dumpster.

She calmly walked out of the alley and onto the sidewalk. As she rounded the corner, heading back to the department store, she heard a large truck come to a stop behind her. Looking back, she saw a sanitation truck turn into the back alley behind the line of shops. Smiling at her luck, she went back to the department store and slipped back in unnoticed.

~*~

"Grandma, look at this one!" Kimberly called from the end of the aisle. "It's just what Kryssi would wear."

"Kimberly Lee Tucker, where have you been?" Jean asked coming over to her granddaughter.

"Right here," Kimberly said with a smile. "I was digging through these shirts."

"So what did you find?" Jean asked. Kimberly held up a powder blue shirt with a collection of fairies on the front and the word "Believe" written below them. "Well, that's pretty," Jean said. "What else do they have?"

"Come and look," Kimberly said. As the little girl drew her grandmother into the racks of shirts, the sound of sirens drew the attention of everyone in the store. Curiosity got the better of Kimberly and Jean when they saw several police cars and an ambulance coming to a stop just outside. The two made their way to the front of the store and joined the crowd who was looking out the window.

As the crowd at the window thickened, someone bumped into Kimberly and nearly knocked her down. She turned to the offender and said, "Excuse me," before looking up to see whom it was.

"Kimberly," her mother said, surprised. "What are you doing here?"

"We just came to get Kryssi some clothes," Jean said from behind her daughter. "What is happening outside?"

"I don't know," Janet said, turning back to the window.

"But, didn't I just see you coming in?"

"I still don't know what's happening," Janet said, avoiding her mother's eyes.

After a few minutes, those closest to the window saw two paramedics wheeling a gurney to the waiting ambulance.

"They've got the head covered," someone said.

Another person whispered, "Oh no."

"They must be dead," a third person offered.

That statement snapped Janet and Jean from their curiosity. "Come on, Kimmy," Jean said. "You don't need to see this."

"Kimberly," the girl corrected, mumbling as she allowed her grandmother to lead her back to the clothing department. Soon, a new buzz went through the patrons at the front and Kimberly looked up to see a police officer had entered the store. While he made his way through the customers and employees, asking them a few questions each, Kimberly and her grandmother had gathered a sizable collection of various clothing for Krystal.

"Of course, we'll get her some more, later," Grandma said as they made their way to the checkout. "But this should do her for a week or more."

"Excuse me," a man said from behind them. Kimberly and her grandmother turned and saw Officer Morrow standing there.

"Oh," Jean said. "You're that nice officer who brought Kimmy home a few weeks ago."

Shane glanced at Kimberly and smiled in recognition. "Yes," he said. "Unfortunately, I have to ask her some questions again, as well as you ma'am."

"Please call me Jean," the older woman said. "I mean if we run into each other much more, I'll have to start setting a place for you at the table."

Shane smiled at the woman's flirtation, and tipped his hat a little. "I hate to ask this ma'am, uh, Jean," he said, changing it when he saw her warning finger come up. "How long have you and Kimmy been in the store here?"

"Kimberly," the girl mumbled.

"About an hour," Jean said just as quickly. "We came to do some shopping."

"Did you notice anything unusual outside as you were coming in, or through the window while you were here?"

"No," Jean said, "At least not until we heard the sirens."

"Do you know a girl named Mindy McDowell?" Shane asked.

Kimberly knew it was a trick. "She's my friend from school," she said. "Well, not so much anymore."

"Why aren't you friends anymore?" Shane asked.

"We're still friends," Kimberly said. "But she hasn't been in school for a while." Kimberly looked up to see an icy stare coming from her grandmother. Unfortunately, Shane saw it as well.

"I take it you know her as well," he said to the older woman.

"I didn't know she was a McDowell," Jean said. "If I did, I certainly wouldn't have..." She paused and looked down at Kimberly. "Kimmy, could you pay for everything for me while I talk to the officer? Do you mind?" the last she said to Shane. While Kimberly waited for the sales clerk to ring up the items, she watched her grandmother talk to officer Morrow. The animated way she spoke told her the woman was telling him precisely what she thought of the McDowell family.

Just as the clerk told her the total, she saw Officer Morrow say something to her grandma, which caused the woman to bring her hand to her lips. Kimberly paid the clerk and took the cart to the front of the store where she waited for her grandma.

Jean was unusually quiet on the trip home. Kimberly asked her what Officer Morrow said, but her grandmother refused to talk about it. When they walked through the door, she handed the bags to Kimberly and told her to run upstairs to put everything away.

As she went upstairs to comply, she heard her grandmother's voice speaking to the rest of the family. After a moment, she heard her Uncle Bob's distinctive voice all but shout, "It's what he deserves for what he did," followed by a chorus of shushes. Kimberly realized that officer Morrow had told her grandma that something awful had happened. It didn't take a genius to figure out what it was.

~*~

Angela woke up and raised her head from the sofa. She looked around her and took an inventory of her surroundings. What she saw disgusted her. Beer bottles, food containers, papers and all manner of trash littered the living room. The smell from the kitchen was making her nauseous. She swung her legs off the sofa and sat up.

"Where's Mindy?" she asked.

"Huh?" Jason asked, not paying attention to her.

"Where is Mindy?" she asked again.

"Went shoppin'," Jason said, turning the volume up on the TV.

"What," Angela asked, "by herself?"

"Christ sake," Jason said. "She's fifteen years old. She can go shoppin' by herself."

"She's ten Jason, and no she can't!"

Jason looked at her incredulous. "Ten," he asked.

"Yes."

"Hell," he said, standing up. "She'll never be able to buy a case of beer." He moved to get his boots and tripped over a Chinese takeout carton. "Ech," he said as he wiped a slimy noodle from his sock. "Why don't you pick this shit up while I go get her?"

After putting his boots on, Jason left the house, slamming the door as he went. Angela winced as the noise sent a spike of pain through her temple. She dragged herself off the sofa and picked her way through the kitchen to get to the broom.

~*~

Keith Rogan had just turned onto Willowood Lane when he saw

the grey pickup barrel through the next intersection. As the Chevy got closer, he made a quick note of the front tags and called it in. He was on a mission, but he still watched the pickup through his rear-view mirror as it sped through that four-way stop as well.

He had gone less than half a block when the dispatcher called back that the vehicle belonged to William McDowell. "Shit," Rogan said as he turned on his lights and made a sharp U-turn. In not time he caught up to the pickup and switched on his siren as well. He saw the person look in his rear-view and shake his head before pulling over.

"Three fifteen to Central," Rogan said into his radio.

"Central," the dispatcher replied.

"Central I have a 10-61 on that 2003 Chevrolet S-10. Subject drove through two intersections before I began pursuit. I received notification that the vehicle belongs to the brother of the individual receiving a courtesy call."

"Ten-four, 315," the dispatcher said. "Captain advises you check for intoxication before advising him of the situation."

"Ten-four Central," Rogan said as he retrieved the breathalyzer from his glove compartment. "This guy's day is about to turn to shit," he said as he got out of the cruiser.

It took a few minutes for Rogan to determine that Jason was below the legal limit, barely. Once he confirmed that fact, he radioed it in to the dispatcher, who gave him permission to deliver the news about his daughter. When Rogan broke the news, the man did something he'd never done in his life. He fainted.

ANIMUS

TEN

Jean stopped at the top of the stairs and took a deep breath. She really did not want to do this, but Janet asked her. She squared her shoulders, took another deep breath and opened the door to her granddaughters' room. Kimberly was busy removing the tag from a shirt when the door opened, so she waited until it fell into the trash before laying the scissors down and looking up.

"Kimmy," Jean said quietly. "Um, can- can you come downstairs for a moment? We need to talk to you."

'This is it,' Kimberly thought as she nodded and rose to follow her grandmother. When the two of them reached the living room, Jean guided Kimberly to the sofa and had her sit down.

"Kimmy," Jean started.

"Kimberly, please, Grandma." The girl said. Jean started and straightened her posture as she too took a seat on the sofa. Kimberly looked around and noticed the faces of all of her family had a somber expression.

"I know," Kimberly said. She refused to show her gratification when the entire family started.

"You know what, sweetheart?" Grandpa Adam asked.

"I know that Mindy's dead," she said.

"How," Jean asked, clearly shaken.

Kimberly looked at the woman. "We saw them putting someone dead in the ambulance," she said. "And Officer Morrow asked us if we knew her. He didn't ask us if we knew anyone else in the family, just her."

"I can't believe we keep forgetting how smart you are," Sue said, tears falling down her face.

"How did it happen?" she asked.

"No one knows, sweetie," Grandpa David said. "The police haven't released the details yet."

"Sweetheart, if you need to talk to anyone…" Grandma Carol began.

"No," Kimberly said. "I-, I just want to finish putting Kryssi's things away."

Grandma Jean looked like she wanted to say more, but her husband stopped her before she could. "Okay Kim-, Kimberly," she said instead.

As Kimberly stood, she looked at her family and noted their concerned looks. "I just want to be alone for a while," she said before turning for the stairs. As she walked through the living room, each family member in her path felt compelled to touch her shoulder or pat her head as she passed.

Once upstairs, she picked up the last shirt and the scissors. She removed the last tag and let it fall into the wastebasket. Once she folded the shirt, she placed it in Krystal's drawer and sat down on the bed. 'What happens now?' she asked herself. She looked out the bedroom window and down the street. She couldn't see the McDowell house from here, but she knew that just a few streets away, chaos is happening in that house. A smile spread across her face. 'Sometimes justice finds a way to serve itself,' she thought.

~*~

Jason walked into the morgue on legs made of jelly, carried by feet made of lead. Everything seemed unreal. He looked at the man who led him in and followed where he indicated.

Once again, his words of mockery to his brother haunted him. He remembered goading his brother for crying over the loss of his wife, but now, for the second time in a month, he was near tears himself. 'There's a million more out there!' his own voice shouted at him. 'A million more!'

"The wound is quite severe," the man said to him. He may as well have been talking to himself. The man lifted the sheet covering the little girl. Jason looked down, saw his little girl's face and closed his eyes. He nodded and turned away.

"There will have to be an autopsy," the man told him as he placed the sheet back over the girl's face. "And you'll have to fill out some forms." Jason walked out of the morgue, paying no heed to the man or his forms.

He stumbled out to his truck and collapsed onto his knees beside it. He leaned his head on the door and cried. He couldn't get the image of his little girl out of his head. He saw the jagged cuts on her neck and the look in her eyes. 'Why didn't they close her eyes?' He cried harder and began beating his fists against the door of his truck.

A couple, leaving the hospital noticed him and gave him a wide berth. He didn't even know they were there. He got tired of punching his truck and his tears were all but dry, still he cried. He leaned back and sat on the pavement. He wanted to go back in there and make them tell him that his daughter wasn't dead. He wanted them to tell him his son wasn't dead. He wanted someone to tell him he was having a really bad dream. He knew he would never get those things he wanted, so he decided to want something he could get. He wanted a drink.

It took him less than five minutes to leave the hospital and find his favorite bar. He went in, fell into a booth and waited for one of the waitresses to come take his order.

Krystal and Janet came home at around nine o'clock. Krystal still had her G-tube in place, but Dr. Satish told her she could have it removed on Tuesday, if she could keep semi-solid food down. If everything went well, by next month, he would finally allow her to have pizza. Within a couple of months, she would have no dietary restrictions. They spent a while allowing the family to fawn over her before Krystal looked around and asked for Kimberly. Grandma Jean told her that her sister was upset and in her room, to which the girl bolted for the stairs.

"Be careful," her mother called after her. "You knock that tube out and it'll take longer for you to get pizza!"

"She's really upset about that girl," Carol said, when Krystal was out of sight. "I know it's awful to say this, but after what that bastard did, I'm surprised you let Kimberly be friends with that girl,"

"She's not her friend, Carol," Janet said. "They're in the same class and Kimberly was tolerating her until she can skip a grade at the end of the year."

"She seems awfully upset for someone who wasn't friends with her," Sue said.

"She's just upset because she's been exposed to all of the stuff that's happened to the McDowell family."

"What stuff," Bob scoffed.

Janet explained to her family about the deaths in Jason McDowell's family. She told them how Kimberly felt responsible because she wished the man would suffer for what he did. She finished by saying, "I think that she blames herself for Mindy's death. She thinks that because she wanted him to suffer, that caused his family to die."

"Come on, Janet," Mike said. "You know she's too smart to believe that."

"Smart, yes," Janet said. "But she's still just eight-years-old. No matter how smart she is, believing something at that age is sometimes more powerful than knowing different."

"Maybe," David said. "Still, aside from the fact that two children are dead, which is a tragedy, the guy deserves all of the suffering he's going through." There was a quiet murmur of agreement from the rest of the family. Janet sighed and leaned back in the sofa.

"I just wish he could be suffering without it affecting Kimberly," she said. The family stayed a while longer, but the day's events had dampened their celebratory mood. Soon, everyone left, with promises of returning the next day to celebrate properly. Janet closed the door when her parents, the last of them, walked out to their car. She looked up the stairs and sighed. Now came the part she least wanted to face.

She climbed the stairs, hoping to hear her daughters' laughter coming from the other side of the door. Unfortunately, all was quiet. She opened the bedroom door and found Kimberly sitting on her bed watching as Krystal tried on her new clothes. Janet was not surprised to see the girl managed to find a way to make her shirts accommodate the tube coming from her belly. She was surprised that Krystal had managed to find odd shoes to wear.

"Seriously?" she asked. "Even now you won't wear matching shoes?" Both girls jumped when they heard their mother's voice. Krystal looked at her mother and adopted a 'sweet and innocent' smile.

"But Mommy," she said. "How will I tell my feet apart if they look the same?" Janet stared wide-eyed at the child, before the ridiculousness of that question hit her. She could not help but laugh at her daughter and walk over to wrap her in a hug.

"Sweetheart," Janet said, after her laughter died. "Mommy needs to talk to Kimberly a minute. Can you wait downstairs?"

"Mommy," Kimberly said, before Krystal could answer. "She should stay. Kryssi needs to hear everything."

"I want to stay, Mommy," Krystal said. Janet sighed. She really did not want to have this conversation at all. She wanted to involve Krystal even less. She looked at her two daughters in turn and finally nodded. She let go of Krystal and allowed the girl to sit on her own bed before going over to the desk and sitting on the edge of it.

"The man who drove that truck, the day you were hurt, lives just a few streets from here," Janet began. "His name is Jason McDowell." Janet shared the whole story with Krystal. She told the girls how Jason avoided punishment, how he lived, if not happily, then at least peacefully for three years without giving the Tuckers a second thought. She told how Kimberly had inadvertently became close to Jason's daughter and how she was there the day Jason's sister-in-law died. The part that surprised Kimberly was when she told them that she was at the McDowell house and she saw Joyce McDowell fall from the roof of her house, that day.

Kimberly took up the story and told her mother and Krystal how she called 9-1-1 that day, but did nothing else to help the woman. She talked about how glad she was to know that someone close to the man who had killed her daddy was dead as well. Between Janet and Kimberly, they managed to tell Krystal everything from that point forward up to today when they learned that someone killed Mindy McDowell.

Of course, no one told the entire story. No one mentioned how JJ, Billy and Mindy McDowell died, though both said they were relieved to know that the McDowell family finally met justice.

When they finished their story, Janet and Kimberly watched Krystal closely for some sign that she understood. Krystal began crying and both her sister and mother were by her side in an instant.

"What's wrong, honey?" Janet asked.

"Can't you two get in trouble for what happened to them?" Krystal asked.

"Oh, honey, no," Janet said. "We didn't have an active part in those people dying. Most of them were accidents. And Mindy, well, we weren't around when Mindy died." Janet and Kimberly soothed Krystal's fears and to a lesser extent, their own as well. A short while later, Janet had the girls tucked into bed and was heading for her own. 'It's been a long, exhausting day,' she thought. 'Was it just this morning that Kryssi woke up?'

She yawned and rubbed her eyes as she entered her bedroom. Sitting on the bed, she began thinking about the McDowell family again. '...and there is so much more to do,' she thought, kicking her door closed.

Jason poured the amber liquid into his mouth and watched as a group of kids started making acting foolish on what this dive called a dance floor. He poured another shot of bourbon and held it up.

"To the dances neither one of you will go to," he said, before throwing the drink into his mouth. The alcohol stopped burning his throat twenty minutes ago, he thought. It might have been longer. It might not have been as long. He didn't care. He poured again, this time raising the glass and saluting the drinks they'd never get to buy.

"It all comes down to one thing," he said to his shadow. "If Angie had stayed home and raised those kids, they wouldn't be dead now." The logic made perfect sense to him. The woman wanted to go to work and doing that, she neglected his kids. She killed his kids. That thought stuck in his head. The more he rolled it around, the more he realized that it had to be true. "I mean I was in the shower," he told the shadow. "She coulda done somethin' to the truck and got Billy and JJ killed. How do I know she didn't slip out and kill Mindy too?"

He thought of the gashes under his little girl's chin. In his mind, he saw Angela taking that damned knife that Billy's whore was so partial to, and stabbing his baby girl in the throat. Each time he saw it, he got angrier. 'That bitch has to pay for what she did.' He thought, grabbing the bottle of bourbon and staggering to his feet. He left the bar and got into his truck.

Jason didn't remember driving home. He sat in the driveway and breathed heavily. He kept seeing his bitch-wife slamming his son's head into the asphalt. He saw her cutting his daughter's head off. He saw her pushing Joyce from the roof. All of these things kept circling his head. He tipped the bourbon to his lips and sucked on the bottle until nothing but air fell into his mouth.

He got out of the truck and flung the bottle, not caring that it sailed across the street and burst in his neighbor's driveway. He made his way to the porch and stumbled up the steps.

~*~

Shane Morrow finished filling out his reports. Typing up all of the witness statements, all of which said they saw nothing, was time consuming and boring. He thought about the email he got earlier. If he hadn't gone to the accident site on Second Avenue, he might have been there to stop the McDowell girl from going to town. 'What was she doing in town by herself?' he asked himself.

He spoke with the detective at the scene and explained the email he received. The detective, not Parris this time, asked him to forward the email. Having done that, Shane wondered what else he could be doing.

For a while, he thought that maybe McDowell himself had killed his sister-in-law and brother. His kids dying didn't make any sense at all. 'Killing his brother got him his brother's house and truck,' Shane thought. 'What does killing his kids get him? There's no insurance, I checked on that.'

Shane went through all of the common motives. An affair didn't make sense. Anyone who would sleep with him wouldn't care if her had kids. The wife didn't seem like the type to mess around. Money wasn't an issue. None of them had any. 'So if it wasn't McDowell, who was it?'

His next thought was the Tucker woman. There was some motive. The problem with her, he believed her when she said she stayed away from McDowell. Then again, one of her relatives could have decided to take justice in their own hands. Would any of them be sick enough to kill his kids? One thing for sure, Shane found that the link between the two families, three years ago and now, was more than a coincidence. His gut told him that much.

Shane got tired of running everything through his mind. Parris was right. He needed evidence, and he could only think of one place he could get it. He logged out of the system and grabbed his keys. 'Screw policy,' he thought. 'I'm going to get some answers.'

His first stop was the crime lab. He went straight to Ben's office to find him going over some reports. Ben glanced up as Shane entered and held up a hand.

"The preliminary results aren't even in yet," Ben said. "I promise to cc you on everything we find.

"I need to ask you something else," Shane said. Ben looked up at him and waited. "What are the odds of someone killing his or her entire family with no motive?"

"There's always a motive," Ben said. "We just don't always know what it is."

"Okay," Shane said. "What are the odds of someone killing his or her entire family with no apparent motive?"

"For women, I would say about 50-55% of all family homicides occur by the mother's hand with no immediately discernible motive. Men, about 30%, but that's just a guess."

"Why such a difference?"

"Women are just more likely to kill their children than men. However, men are more likely to kill their spouses than women."

"Okay," Shane said. "I don't need a CSI. I need you to make a personal guess. Do you think that the members of the McDowell family are being killed by a family member or someone else?"

Ben sighed and leaned back in his chair. "I can't answer that," he said.

"Why not?" Shane asked.

"Because you will take what I say and go off looking for something to prove it right. That's not how to handle an investigation."

"Screw that!" Shane said. "I need to know where to look. Everywhere I turn there is something that says 'yes he did it,' but something else that says, 'no, it was her.'"

"So you suspect that one of the parents killed their children and the others."

"I don't know who to suspect. They don't have motive, but there is a lot of evidence. The other people I suspect have motive, but no evidence."

"I hate to quote TV," Ben said. "But in my world, you follow the evidence."

~*~

She opened the door and peered inside. The soft snores told her the entire house was asleep. After quietly closing the bedroom door, she slipped downstairs and out the back door. She jogged the entire distance to Willowood Lane.

Once on the street, she slowed to a brisk walk. She was three houses away when she heard glass breaking across the street. She stopped cold until she realized McDowell himself had thrown something over there. She crept forward and saw him as he stumbled up the steps. Just as she made it to the edge of the yard, he kicked the door ferociously.

She ran to the other side of the house, so she could see inside the living room as he barged in. "You fuckin' did it!" she heard him scream as he lunged for the woman on the sofa. The woman didn't have a chance to get out of the way before he was on her.

"You pushed Joyce off the roof!" he yelled, emphasizing the accusation with a tug on the woman's hair. He slapped her in the face and spat on her. "You killed my boy!" This he followed with a punch to the woman's stomach. "You killed Billy!" he shouted, punching her in the face. "You killed Mindy!"

She watched ad McDowell punched his wife in the face again and let her slump to the floor. She ducked down as he spun to face her direction. She heard him stomp closer to the window and her heart began thumping. A moment later, she heard him stomp away and chanced another peek into the house. She saw him raise an aluminum bat and bring it crashing down on his wife's back. She winced, feeling a slight sympathy pain.

Jason brought the bat back again, underhanded, this time. He swung it like a golf club and it slammed into the woman's ribs. Just as he was about to swing again, headlights appeared a few houses down.

She ducked around the corner of the house and waited for the car to pass, but it didn't. She nearly let out a squeal as she saw the police car stop in front of McDowell's house. She crept further into the shadows, trying to hide from the cop's sight.

A sudden shattering sound came from above her and glass rained down. She looked up to see the bloody face of Angela

McDowell hanging out of the window above her. She scrambled back further until she came to the back of the house.

She heard the officer shout out, "What's going on here?" The last thing she saw before disappearing around the corner was Angela being dragged back into the house just as the officer came around the side.

'I have to get out of here,' she thought. She jumped over the back fence and ran through the neighbor's yard. As she ran around that house, she made it to the street. 'This is…' she thought, trying to remember the name of the street. 'Winwood, that's it.'

She ran down Winwood Lane to where it crossed Pine Street. She turned left and circled back to Willowood Lane. She saw the flashing lights of the police car and neighbors starting to emerge from their homes. Her time was up. She had to go.

She casually crossed Pine Street and walked back towards Winwood, before slipping into someone's yard and disappearing behind their house. She knew, thankfully that there were no fences between here and her house. She ran as fast as she could through the yards and dashed across streets until she came to her house. She collapsed onto her knees in her back yard and stayed there, panting until she got her breath back.

Still breathing somewhat hard, she went to her back door and eased it open. She slipped into the house and quietly closed and locked the back door. Just as she was turning around and getting ready to slip back upstairs, the kitchen light came on. She froze on the spot. Krystal was standing there in the kitchen staring at her.

"Where were you?" the girl asked.

~*~

Jason dragged his wife's body back inside. He wasn't done with her yet. "Please," she whimpered as he held her up by the throat.

The simple request fueled his anger rather than abated it. He slapped her hard across the face as he held her upright by her hair. "Did Mindy say please when you cut her head off?" he shouted.

"Wha-" she was cut off by a hard punch to the stomach that knocked the breath from her. She wasn't sure, but she thought he said something about Mindy. 'What happened to my baby?' she asked herself before his knee connected with her cheek.

Jason was so angry with her, he started seeing red. His anger increased until blue started flashing in front of his eyes. He dragged her by the throat into the kitchen. She tried to reach up, to pry his hand off her throat, but he grabbed her wrist and slammed it onto the edge of the counter. A sudden wave of nausea told her, her wrist was broken. He dragged her to the sink and began rummaging around on the counter. He found what he was looking for, exactly where Joyce always kept it.

"You didn't even bother to hide it?" he asked her through gritted teeth, jerking her head to the sink and slamming it hard on the edge.

She struggled to stand, to get some leverage, to ease the suffocating grasp he had on her windpipe, but he kicked at her and was gratified to feel something snap. He looked down and saw her leg angled all wrong. He pulled her back into the living room and threw her into the hall. She tried to get up as he stalked to her. She made it to her knee as her broken leg stuck out to her side. She looked up at him in time to see the sole of his work boot slam into her face. Her head snapped back and she felt something break. She had just enough left in her to hope it was the bannister.

He reached down and grabbed her again by the throat before he pulled her into a standing position. She tried to hop into a stable position on her one good leg.

"Police, don't move!" she heard someone shout.

"Fuck You!" Jason answered. Angela felt something slide across her neck, followed by something warm and wet being poured over her neck and chest. She heard a loud pop, and then nothing else.

~*~

"Three-oh-eight to Central," Officer Shane Morrow shouted into his radio as he flipped his switch to turn on his emergency lights. "I have a possible 10-64, domestic disturbance at 4-2-7 Willowood Lane One subject badly beaten, request an ambulance and backup code 10-33."

"Ten-four, 308," the dispatcher said. "Ambulance and backup are en-route, E.T.A. is five minutes. Try to diffuse the situation."

"Ten-four," Shane said as he drew his sidearm. He approached the house cautiously. He saw through the open door as a body was hurled into the hall and it struck the stairs. He climbed the porch steps and approached the door just as someone slammed their foot into the face of their victim.

When he saw the man lift, what appeared to be a woman up by the throat, he breached the entrance of the house. He trained his weapon on the suspect and shouted, "Police, don't move!"

The man, Jason McDowell, he could now see looked up at him and answered, "Fuck you!" before slicing the butcher knife across the woman's throat. Shane fired his weapon, hitting McDowell in the arm that held the knife.

Husband and wife fell simultaneously and Shane lunged for the woman, hoping to catch her. He knelt on the floor in the hall and held his hand on the neck wound, trying his best to slow the blood flow until the ambulance arrived. He knew he was fighting a losing battle, but he tried nonetheless. As he watched the woman's life flow from her, he felt a movement in front of him.

Shane let the dead woman fall to the floor as he lunged at her killer. He had McDowell covered with his own body and wrestled the man onto his stomach. After a brief struggle, Shane cinched the handcuffs in place and started draggin McDowell back into the living room. Once he had his suspect immobilized, he reached for the radio, clipped to his shoulder.

"Three-oh-eight to Central," he said between his heavy breaths. Notify medical examiner and CSI to this scene. I have one fatality, female, age roughly thirty years. She has a large neck wound. Suspect is male, roughly the same age with a G.S.W. to the left arm. He is restrained and in custody."

"Ten-four, 308," the dispatcher answered. "M.E. and CSI are en-route, Shift Captain and detectives as well."

Shane Morrow stood in the living room and stared at the man sitting in the floor. He looked behind him at the body of Angela McDowell. He couldn't wrap his mind around why a man would kill his entire family. He heard more sirens approaching and let out a sigh. He looked down at his weapon and for one brief moment, considered the unthinkable.

He was spared his decision by the arrival of Keith Rogan, followed by two paramedics. The medics tried, unsuccessfully to revive Angela while Rogan stood by Shane's side and waited for everyone else.

~*~

Still breathing somewhat hard, she went to her back door and eased it open. She slipped into the house and quietly closed and locked the back door. Just as she was turning around and getting ready to slip back upstairs, the kitchen light came on. She froze on the spot. Krystal was standing there in the kitchen staring at her.

"Where were you?" the girl asked.

She always hated the hip, cool little catchphrases the kids used. Sadly, in this particular moment, the only thing that she could think of was the single word: 'Busted!'

She looked at Krystal and leveled a gaze at her. "What are you doing up?" she asked.

"I got thirsty," Krystal said. "I went to wake you up to come down and get something to drink with me, but you weren't in your bed."

"I stepped out," she said.

"But where," Krystal asked.

"I don't have to tell you that," she said.

"Okay," Krystal said. "Maybe you can tell Mom."

"You wouldn't dare," she said, coming around the counter to catch up to her sister.

Krystal turned around and smiled. "No," she said. "But I still want to know where you went."

"Okay," she said, "But tomorrow. Right now, I just want a drink and to go to bed."

"No," Krystal said. "Tell me where you went, now, and tomorrow you can give me the details."

She sighed as she opened the refrigerator. Three years can do a lot to a person. For instance, she forgot how stubborn her twin sister could be. She also forgot that she inevitably always gave in and let Kryssi have her way. "Fine," she said, pulling out to apple juice boxes and handing one to her sister. "I went to Mindy's."

"Why?"

"Details tomorrow, remember?"

"That was before-"

"And too bad, you made the arrangement," she said, interrupting the other girl. She noticed Krystal's pout and resolved herself not to fall for the guilt. "Look, I promise, I'll tell you everything tomorrow. But you have to promise never to tell anyone."

"I promise," Krystal said, taking a sip from her juice box. Kimberly turned off the light and she and Krystal went back upstairs to their bedroom. It had been a long day for both of them, for very different reasons. Still, as tired as they were, neither girl fell asleep right away. The each lay in their beds thinking about the events of the day.

Kimberly waited until she heard her sister begin snoring before getting out of bed and going back downstairs. She went to the living room and pulled the note with Mindy's login information from its hiding place before taking it to the downstairs bathroom to flush it.

She came back to the living room and sat on the sofa, making a mental list of everything she did to Jason McDowell and his family. She checked off everything she used and made sure that she disposed of each item properly. By two o'clock, she felt confident there was no evidence linking her or her family to the killings. In fact, with the police catching Jason in the act of trying to kill his wife, she doubted they would look for anything more.

She lay back on the sofa and thought about each killing and how it made her feel. Then she remembered that she would have to tell Krystal everything the next day. The last thought Kimberly had before she eventually fell asleep was, 'Tomorrow is going to be one big mess.'

~*~

EPILOGUE

"Okay girls," John Tucker said as they came back downstairs from serving his wife breakfast in bed. "Who wants to go with me to pick up Mommy's birthday cake?"

"I do, I do," Krystal squealed as she jumped up and down.

John looked at his other daughter who simply grabbed up a Dr. Seuss book and headed into the living room. Kimberly had started reading two years ago, a full year and a half before her twin sister. Since then, it became all she wanted to do. John and Janet Tucker found it an ever-increasing struggle to keep Kimberly's reading material age appropriate. "Kimberly?" he asked.

"I'm just going to read, Daddy," the little girl said as she sat on the sofa.

"Okay," John said. "We'll be back in about twenty minutes."

"Okay," Kimberly said, with a nod, only half hearing him as he and her sister walked out the door.

"If we're not," John said getting her attention. "I need you to kill them all."

"What?" Kimberly said as her book dropped into the floor.

"Kill everyone he loves and make him suffer like he makes you and your mommy suffer," John said.

"Daddy, I-"

"I know you can do it baby," John said, "You're the only one strong enough to do it."

Kimberly sat bolt upright. Her heart was pounding and she chanced a look over the back of the sofa. Thankfully, her father wasn't there, but his command from her dream lingered. 'Kill them all,' still rang through her head as she looked down into the floor to find a Dr. Seuss book. "I did, Daddy," she whispered. She bent to pick up the book. It was the same one she was reading that day.

"How did this get here?" she asked.

"How did what get here?" Janet asked, causing Kimberly to nearly jump out of her skin.

"This book."

"Hm," Janet said looking over her daughter's shoulder. "Kryssi must have left it there last night. You better get dressed. We're taking Kryssi to the park for a while." Janet barely got the words out of her mouth when the telephone rang and she picked it up. "Hello," she said.

"Janet," Jean said from the other end of the line. "Turn on your TV to any local channel."

"Why?"

"They arrested the bastard last night."

"What?"

"They think he killed his whole family. They caught him in the act killing his wife!"

Janet dropped the telephone and ran to the living room. She snatched up the remote and turned the TV on.

"Here you see a deranged and obviously intoxicated Jason McDowell being led from his home last night," the local newscaster was saying. "He was taken to Piedmont Memorial Hospital, where he was treated for a gunshot wound to the arm. He is in stable condition, but under heavy guard.

"McDowell is suspected of killing both his brother and son by tampering with the brakes on his own truck and then making his brother use his truck to pick up dinner. JJ McDowell died on impact in a wreck that same night, Jason's brother William a few days later. Police also suspect him of murdering his own daughter just yesterday, although they still lack the evidence to prove those charges.

"Recapping the top story, Jason McDowell was arrested last night for murder. He was taken into custody after a patrol officer from the Piedmont Acres Police Department witnessed him killing his own wife. Police are asking the public if they know of anything that can help them close the open murder of McDowell's daughter yesterday, to please come forward."

Janet stared at the TV in shock. Kimberly looked from the screen to her mother, then back again. She couldn't believe it. He was finally being punished. "Holy crap," the two of them heard from the stairs. Krystal looked from her mother to her sister in total disbelief.

Three hours later, Kimberly and Krystal were at the nearly deserted park. Everyone else their age was at school, so except for a few little kids, they had the place to themselves. Kimberly looked over at her mother as she finished her story.

"So, when I saw the cop coming around the house, I ran back

home," she said.

Krystal looked at her sister and brought her swing to a stop. "You did all of that just to get me to wake up?" she asked.

"And because someone had to make him suffer," Kimberly said, bringing her own swing to a halt. Krystal came over to her sister and wrapped her arms around Kimberly's neck.

"I love you," she whispered.

~*~

Thursday, August 28, 2014 – 01:25 pm:

"Does the jury have a verdict?" Judge Eric Dunlap asked. A man in the jury box rose and handed a piece of paper to the bailiff.

"We have, Your Honor," he said. The judge read the note and handed it back to the bailiff, who returned it the jury foreman.

Judge Dunlap looked at the jury and asked, "In the matter before you, the case of the people versus Jason McDowell on the first charge of murder in the first degree, how do you find the defendant?"

"Guilty, Your Honor"

"In the matter stated above, on the second charge of murder in the first degree, how do you find the defendant?"

"Guilty,"

The words struck a blow to Jason and he seemed to crumble each time he heard the word. Four counts of murder. Four guilty verdicts. By the time the final verdict came, Jason was leaning on the table for support. His wife, his children, his brother, all dead and he had no idea how it all happened.

As the deputies led him from the courtroom, three pairs of eyes followed him. Below those eyes, three mouths turned up as smiles spread across their faces.

~*~

Friday, August 29, 2014 – 10:30 am:

Janet sat across the desk from the bald man in the cheap suit. She was livid. She had worked so hard avoiding this, only to be told it was all for nothing.

"I'm sorry, Mrs. Tucker," the man said. "But we really have no choice. The bank will foreclose on your house at ten o'clock on Monday if you do not have the $15,000 by the end of business today." As Janet rose to leave the bank, the bald man called after her, "Please remember, Mrs. Tucker, you are prohibited from removing any furniture or appliances from the home! The result will be criminal prosecution."

Janet walked out of the man's office with her daughters trailing behind her. She didn't realize that Kimberly stopped and turned back to the bald man and gave him a look of pure hatred.

ABOUT THE AUTHOR

Thomas Evans is a Criminal Justice professional and an avid reader with a vivid imagination. His first books, a group of children's stories, show how his autistic granddaughter sees the world around her. The Hannah books have been well received by readers. Thomas Also contributes to the online satire news magazine, Bloid News, where he writes articles endorsing and supporting fellow authors and their latest works. He currently lives with his wife, two daughters and granddaughter in North Carolina.

CONNECT WITH THOMAS

WEBSITE: http://www.fanficcollection.com/

BLOG: http://tevans41.blogspot.com/

TWITTER: https://twitter.com/tevans71

8429850R00145

Printed in Great Britain
by Amazon.co.uk, Ltd.,
Marston Gate.